Praise for *The Sixth Storm*

"Skye's search for answers to the peculiar weather lashing her coastal town leads her down a dark path, where she's forced to confront her family's tragic past. The story's grip tightens as every discovery leads Skye closer to the edge, leaving the reader to wonder if finding the truth will be the last thing she ever does. A captivating read laden with perils of both the natural and supernatural, balanced with good old-fashioned adventure and heart."

—S.A. Bodeen, author of *The Raft*

"The paranormal curse in the Findlings' The Sixth Storm resonates precisely because the other elements of the story feel so real. Starfish Cove may be fictional, but I've driven through a dozen towns like it on the Oregon Coast, and Skye may be fictional, but we've all known a tenacious young person who refused to give up in the face of difficulties adults couldn't fully understand. This novel will make you feel like you're trapped in a house on the Oregon Coast during an epic storm, and the story is so intriguing, you'll be glad you're there!"

—Benjamin Gorman
author of *Don't Read This Book*
and the bestseller *Corporate High School*

to hannah —

THE
SIXTH
STORM

♡ *Kem*
& Libby ♡

KIM COOPER FINDLING
& LIBBY FINDLING

The Sixth Storm
copyright © Kim Cooper Findling and Libby Findling
2019
First Edition

Paperback ISBN: 978-1-945587-32-0
Library of Congress Control Number: 2019900852
Findling, Kim Cooper and Findling, Libby
The Sixth Storm
1. Fiction; 2. Mystery; 3. Oregon Coast; 4. Family Curse; 5. Mt. Hood; 6. Storms.
Book design: Todd Griffith, Dancing Moon Press
Cover design: Tim Green
Author photograph: Alex Jordan
Manufactured in the United States of America
Dancing Moon Press
www.dancingmoonpress.com

DANCING
MOON
PRESS

Dedication

For the real Beckendorfs
Our ancestors, who arrived in Oregon in 1913

And for Maris and Katherine
Our sisters, who we hope will stay close

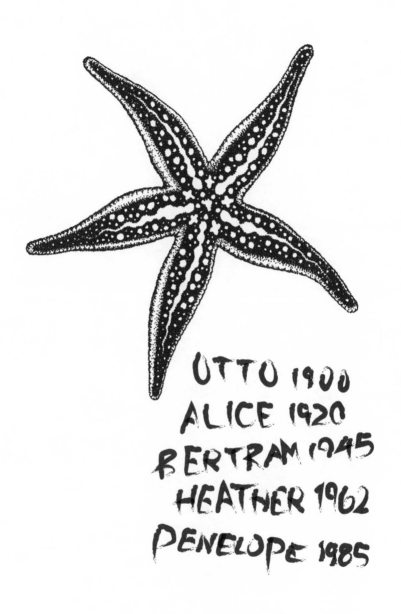

OTTO 1900
ALICE 1920
BERTRAM 1945
HEATHER 1962
PENELOPE 1985

MONDAY, JANUARY 4, 1999

3:07 P.M.

There were only a few days until the anniversary of the storms. Skye Clancy pushed open the steel doors of Starfish Cove Secondary School and ticked through a quick list of what not to think about. She would not think about her Aunt Penelope, or any of the other Dead Beckendorfs. She would not think about her mother, and how sad she was that all her relatives were dead. Most of all, Skye would not think about her birthday, which had nothing to do with her mother's dead family except that they ruined it every year.

Instead, she would think about the sky. Skye looked up. Overhead resembled an open parachute of baby blue, dotted with puffy cumulus clouds gliding south. She loved the weather, its power and contradictions. It could be predicted, but remained unpredictable; it was otherworldly, but had a big impact on the ordinary world. The clouds were cotton-ball-white, not campfire-ash-white or nickel-gray-white, which could indicate rain. Jerry Petrichor had been right. The atmospheric pressure

1

remained stable on the Oregon Coast, and it was a clear and sunny winter afternoon.

Skye bent to tighten the laces on her black Converse sneakers. Her curly blond hair slid around her shoulders and floated in the breeze in the same direction as the clouds. She pulled an elastic off her wrist to make a ponytail, zipped up her grey hoodie, and galloped down the concrete steps past clusters of students towards the beach.

Maybe this January would be different. Maybe Skye's mother wouldn't get so sad. It was four days into the month, and so far Veronica seemed okay. Next week was fourteen years since Veronica's twin sister Penelope Beckendorf had vanished in a vicious storm. Had that given grief enough time to take whatever it needed and go away?

Skye caught herself. *Don't think about Penelope!* Maybe if she didn't, her mother wouldn't either.

Skye spotted her brother, Andrew, walking with a dark-haired girl towards his Honda. Andrew was a sophomore, newly in possession of a driver's license and a girlfriend, and the days when her 16-year-old brother went to the beach with his 13-year-old sister seemed to be ancient history. Skye gave a wave in his direction, but he didn't notice. Skye's best friend, Ashley, disappeared after the last bell, too. Ashley wasn't a fan of the wildness of the beach. She greeted the surf spray, the wind, even the sand as personal attacks. For beach trips, Ashley was out.

But Skye was in. She had no problem being alone, either. Every day, she left the commotion of school behind in favor of the half-moon beach of Starfish Cove. She jogged to a narrow trail that cut over the dune and climbed towards the smell of salt and the roar of the ocean. At the surf line, frothy waves rolled onto sand the color of bleached clamshells. The surface was firm beneath her feet and she quickened her pace.

Ahead were the Old Docks, a bunch of rotting timbers stabbed into the sea. She thought one of the Dead Beckendorfs used to launch his fishing boat from the Old Docks. Skye didn't know his name, but how would she, since no one was allowed to talk about her mom's family. No one could speak their names or talk about their lives or, most of all, ask how they died.

Supposedly, the stories were all too terrible to bear. But they weren't going to come back to life, no matter what anyone did, so wasn't it better to understand what had happened? Why couldn't someone investigate the whole stupid family tree and every horrid detail, just get the truth out there?

Stop it! Skye caught herself. *Don't. Think. About. The Dead Beckendorfs!* The truth was a terrible idea, anyway. Just say "Beckendorf" out loud and watch her mother spiral into sorrow.

Skye gazed at the tide pools ahead at the base of the rugged north cliffs. If only she could stay on the beach forever. She dragged herself up and over the dune to Lewis Street, where the roaring of the surf was replaced by her pounding heartbeat. Her sense of dread grew as she passed soggy lawns and scrappy houses until she spotted her own, on the corner of Lewis and Clark. She hopped up onto the cracked curb, balancing as if she was walking a tightrope that might give out beneath her. *Please let Mom not be sad this year. Please don't let me find her home alone and sad.*

Her mother's blue sedan was out front; no sign of her brother's faded silver Honda or her dad's ancient Ford truck. The scene was tired and quiet, but that was nothing new. It wasn't the broken-down cottage that made Skye's belly crunch up. It was the curtains. They were drawn. All of them, closed up against this beautiful day.

Maybe it was nothing—perhaps her mother was in the garden, trimming her purple rhododendron, and had simply forgotten to open the blinds today. Or she was in the kitchen, sketching near the large window. Or she wasn't home at all—she'd walked up to the library.

Or maybe all the blinds were closed because the darkness had returned. Skye's Converse crunched on the gravel drive while her mind raced with all the things she had sworn she wouldn't think about but had thought about anyway. She tiptoed up the front steps and put an ear to the door. Only silence. Skye took a deep breath and turned the knob.

Daylight slid into the room in an arc, illuminating a figure curled in a ball on the couch. Skye shut the door and the light retreated. The room was like a foggy moonless night. Leopold the cat brushed against her legs, releasing a mournful mewl. Skye kicked off her shoes and went to her mother, bending to kiss her on the head.

"Hey, Mom," Skye said.

"Hey, sweetie," her mother whispered. The tracks of leftover tears glistened on her cheeks.

"I'm going to make you tea." Veronica didn't respond.

Skye moved into the gloomy kitchen, where she put the dented kettle on to boil. She opened the curtains and gazed into the side yard. The rhododendron had one bloom lingering amidst its shiny green leaves, but the flower hung limp and mushy.

Skye should have known this was coming. It was no surprise the darkness would return. The darkness came every year, sneaking up like a big shadow monster that tried to eat her family alive. It didn't seem like one person's grief could take down a whole household, but Skye knew by now that grief was always the hungriest member at the dinner table.

The kettle began to howl, but Skye stayed by the window. The sky remained as blue as the sea on a summer day—that was the good news. The mom-darkness had arrived, and Skye knew it would stay right through the date Penelope had vanished. The only thing that would make it worse was a storm.

TUESDAY, JANUARY 5, 1999

7:14 A.M.

Skye's birthday was in seven days. She crept out of the house before dawn and scurried in the dusky gloom towards the beach. She needed to get a glimpse of the sky before anyone else did. Last night on the KTSC weather report, weatherman Jerry Petrichor forecasted light showers moving into the cove late this morning. Nothing of note in a town that received 75 inches of rain a year, and certainly nothing that might send her mother into a panic.

Lewis Street was quiet and dark. It was just bad luck that Skye had been born three days before her aunt died. Majorly terrible luck, mostly for her aunt, of course, but also for Skye, because all her mother could think about on her birthday was Penelope, storms and death, which meant she definitely was not thinking about cake, presents and balloons for her only daughter.

It wasn't raining, not yet. The air was moist and shot through with a winter's chill. Skye climbed up the dune into sand that still held the cold of night. Her parents had turned in early last night. She'd heard them talking in the bedroom until late. Their voices were muted, her dad's careful and pleading, her mother's choked full of sorrow. Skye couldn't hear what they were saying, but she didn't need to. She'd heard it all before. Her father would soothe and plead, but her mother was unreachable. Andrew had not come home at all, not before Skye went to bed, anyway. Maybe her brother had sensed the return of the mom-darkness and chosen to stay away.

Skye paused at the top of the dune. She glanced over her shoulder and then surveyed the beach. There was rarely anyone out this early, but it was creepy to be out alone at dawn and she was reluctant to stray too far from home. A sliver of light was visible to the east, hinting at the rise of the sun. A trio of swollen clouds emerged from blackness to glow with a deep purple-grey hue. Daybreak illuminated the tips of waves coursing evenly towards the shore. Everything seemed as calm as Jerry had projected. With relief, Skye inhaled one more deep breath of sea air before turning on her heel to hurry back to the cottage.

Then, a grumbling at her back.

Skye whirled and faced the ocean. She squinted at the shoreline. Water surged suddenly in an unsettled sea. The gentle light had shifted to purple shot through with ugly grey, as if the sunrise were fighting with the bottomless dark of the nighttime ocean. A silvery sheet of rain sprang into view over the ocean and began moving towards shore, fast. Then, a growl, louder and closer this time.

Skye fell back a few steps. The wall of rain reached the beach in seconds. A curtain of droplets moved up the beach towards her, jabbing angry polka dots into the sand. Skye searched the horizon for an explanation. BOOM! A crash of thunder rocked the earth. A jagged white-hot lightning bolt slammed into the churning sea, lighting up the rugged shoreline for a fast second before the whole scene fell to that creepy light again, the color of a bruise. Another thunderclap threw Skye to the ground. She clamped her hands over her ears.

Thunderstorms were uncommon at the beach, much more likely to form in the mountains than near the sea. Thunderstorms require unstable air, and Jerry hadn't reported that. The length of time between a lightning bolt and a thunderclap determined how far away a thunderstorm was. This storm not only came crashing out of nowhere, it was ridiculously close as well. Another boom sounded, followed immediately by a lightning bolt that shot to the beach like a spear on fire.

Skye ran. She slid down the dune and crashed to the pavement of Lewis Street, her Converse slipping on wet sand. Her heart pounded and her legs churned. The street before her flashed white hot as another lightning bolt chased her home.

Ahead, the cottage was illuminated in that ugly purplish light. Her mother's sedan and her father's truck were parked in the driveway—but where was Andrew's Honda?

She sprinted across the drive as ice-cold daggers of rain pelted her head. She threw open the door and fell inside, slamming her hand over her mouth. *Don't make a sound. Please let Mom be in bed with a pillow over her head.* Down the hallway, her parent's door was closed. Andrew's door was cracked open, but she couldn't see in from this angle. No sounds of movement, and then, behind her, rocks hitting glass.

Skye threw open the curtains and swiped at the water that dripped down her face. A slurry of gigantic hailstones hit the concrete patio with such force that they went right back up towards the sky. What was happening? At the beach, hail was as unlikely as thunderstorms. The cedars in the front yard swayed wildly as another lightning bolt raced to the ground. The onslaught of hail battered the old shake roof, the whole world gone gray and white with banging and hammering.

Behind the wall of hail, towards shore, clear blue. The hail swept over the little cottage in a clattering frenzy, chased by nothing but a flawless sky. Skye waited. She watched. Silence. Blue sky. A bird chirped uncertainly from the side yard.

Skye scrambled for the remote and switched on the TV, keeping the volume low. Jerry Petrichor stood for the 8 a.m. forecast in a flawless blue shirt before the green screen map of the northern Oregon Coast.

"Good morning, Starfish Cove!" he announced with his usual confidence. He said the same thing every day, but this time, he sounded like he'd had a triple espresso chased with chocolate bars for breakfast.

"Today, I have the most interesting job in town," he continued, skittering back and forth across the screen. "You wouldn't know it if you haven't gotten out of bed yet, but Starfish Cove has been experiencing the most remarkable weather."

"Beginning just a few minutes ago, hailstones of exceptional scope began falling," Jerry continued. "And who among you witnessed that incredible show of lightning and thunder at dawn? That was a doozy of a thunderstorm, not to mention very uncommon weather behavior for this region. And the storm went just as quickly as it came."

Skye's heart slammed. She glanced towards the hall again; her mother was going to freak out. Was this how the storms of 1985 had begun, the storms that took Penelope?

Jerry gestured at the weather map. Dark green and purple swept over Starfish Cove and vanished. The screen switched to video replay, and the wicked lightning bolts Skye had seen struck the ocean all over again. On TV, the lightning looked gorgeous and dangerous. Skye wanted to reach for it, but recoiled at the same time.

"None of this was forecast," Jerry said. "And despite what just took place, the prediction for the rest of the day remains calm with little rain."

Skye heard footsteps and whipped around to see her parents standing in the hall. David's eyes were amazed but Veronica's face was white and pinched. Right before her mother turned and fled the room, her blue eyes welled with a pool of tears.

TUESDAY, JANUARY 5, 1999
8:56 A.M.

Skye arrived in Science class and slid into her seat. She opened her notebook, but her mind was miles away from tidal zone bio-organisms. She'd looked for Andrew everywhere. She wanted to talk to him about their mother, and the storm. Where had he gone? But he wasn't in the band room or at his locker. Not in the halls, either.

Ashley walked into class as the bell rang with her multicolored backpack hanging from one arm, a smoothie in danger of spilling tucked under the other arm, and her jacket on inside out. A junk show, as usual.

"Hey, Skye," she said with a grin. Then, apologetically, "Mom left early."

Ashley was an only child and her mom went to work at the TV station early most mornings, but Skye wasn't sure that accounted for the fact that Ashley never managed to get to their locker before the first bell and typically arrived in 1st period carting some semblance of breakfast and appearing like she'd gotten dressed with her eyes closed. A whole passel of siblings and a bunch of parents probably wouldn't make any difference in the personality of Ashley.

"Hey," Skye said. "You're about to dump your smoothie down your pants."

Ashley looked at her cheetah leggings, which were already speckled with a few pink dribbles. "Dang, my new pants!" Her wild red hair was pulled into a messy ponytail and her aviator glasses were fogged over. She slumped into a chair and plunked the smoothie on her desk just in time to avert disaster. She took a swipe at one of the smoothie dribbles on her pants with a hot-pink polished fingernail and then stuck her finger in her mouth.

Skye thought about asking Ashley if she'd seen the storm this morning, but she had a feeling her friend's response would involve a whole lot of *huh?*

As Mr. Flynn gathered worksheets from yesterday's field trip, Skye gazed out the window. The room smelled of damp clothing on teenage bodies, with hints of gasoline from the old furnace and the tang of seawater from the aquarium in the corner. The classroom faced west, but the dune blocked the view of the ocean, so all Skye could see was the blustery sky.

Her dad had dropped her off on his way to the golf course, since Andrew and his Honda were nowhere to be seen. The hail had stopped, but a punishing rain took its place. David navigated the streets carefully, the truck's old tires sliding across the slurry of hailstones. After the newscast, Veronica crawled back in bed. Skye hadn't said a word to either parent about being on the beach this morning—that would not have been a bright idea. During the short drive to school, Skye's father was quiet, and the

12

two did not talk about her mother or anything else.

Now, giant wet streaks of Oregon Coast's finest slid down the windows. She thought about how Jerry had said the forecast was for calm weather as she watched rain pool into glistening puddles in the parking lot. Flashes of this morning played in her head. The lightning. The churning surf. Running for home. Her mother's face.

"What about that storm, hey, people?" In the time she'd been daydreaming, Mr. Flynn had moved on from the field trip to the very thing she'd been pondering herself. He clapped his hands together with glee. "Never seen that on the Oregon Coast, right?"

In fact, Skye knew, someone *had* seen that on the Oregon Coast. Thunderstorms and hail were rare, but almost any weather event could occur at the beach. Coastlines were the most volatile places on earth. Where ocean currents and wind over land and sea collided, all kinds of chaos was possible. Consider what meteorologists called the 100-year-storms, or 50-year-storms—systems that only came along once in a while, but made a lasting impression. There were the storms of 1985, so relevant to her own family, and others as well. Typhoons, tsunamis, a good old-fashioned tempest—go back in time far enough and all of it had occurred on the Oregon Coast.

Not that Skye would dream of contradicting Mr. Flynn. She rarely said a word in class. It wasn't that she didn't understand what was going on. It just seemed easier to keep her mouth shut. Skye glanced at Ashley, hoping her friend wouldn't blurt out some wild suggestion that Skye chime in about her favorite subject. But Ashley was doodling a very elaborate unicorn on her folder and not paying attention to Mr. Flynn or Skye.

A lightning bolt slashed through the sky on the far side of the dune, and the kids in class that were paying attention twitched at the sudden flash of light. Mr. Flynn halted mid-sentence and stared through the window. Thunder boomed overhead and the school walls shook. Ashley jerked, splashing smoothie on the sleeve of her still-inside-out-jacket. "Dang," she muttered.

Skye felt a jolt of excitement mixed with a creepy sense of confusion. The storm was back. But that didn't make any sense. Weather at the beach changed quickly. Especially thunderstorms—they didn't hang around. They moved through. The storm from this morning wouldn't be lurking offshore, stuck in place. And it definitely wouldn't move away and then come back. Wherever the freak thunderstorm from this morning had come from, it should have been long gone.

4

OCTOBER 11, 1900
OTTO BECKENDORF

At dawn, Otto the fisherman trudged along the beach at Starfish Cove just above the surf line. His awkward rubber boots went schlump-splat as he headed for the dock and his trusty boat, Charlotte, to set out for a day of salmon fishing.

He carried two tin buckets, one that held his day's bait and another covered with a cloth that contained his lunch—a bit of fish stew and a chunk of bread left over from last night's supper, packed up by his wife, Marion. Perhaps she had hidden a chunk of cheddar in there, as well, as she knew it pleased him.

The beach grass glittered with last night's dew, but the sky was clear of clouds and as calm as it ever was on the wild Oregon Coast. Otto had selected his lighter woolens this morning and a small knit cap to tug over his ears against the wind on the sea.

A pink sunrise lingered in the sky, and the air was salty and cool on this fine October day. The wealthy tourists who summered at the fancy hotel were gone for the season and the town was quiet once more. Otto was astonished at the effort and money invested to cater to summer visitors. The railroad tracks had been laid from Portland in 1890, and the grand Hotel Starfish Cove built a few years later. The hotel was in view now, perched on the north cliffs, a marvelous stone and wooden structure with an enormous wrap-around porch offering views of the sea.

He couldn't relate to the wealthy visitors, but Otto did understand a desire to be by the sea. He had been in Starfish Cove since he was a little boy, when his family emigrated from Germany. Now, he lived with Marion and their little one, Wolfie, who was but 18 months old, and Marion was expecting their second child early next year.

Otto loved this little town, and he could understand why the visitors did, too. In any case, their lust for the good life included a desire for fresh seafood, which kept Otto busy and brought him money during the busy season.

The silvery-grey of dawn was morphing to the cottony-white of morning. Charlotte was tied securely to the dock ahead. Otto scanned for others, but no one else was out yet that morning. The hour was too early for the dock fishermen or crab netters, and Otto saw no sign of that crazy old Norwegian Sven, his fiercest fishing competitor.

The number of fish in the sea wasn't the source of the competition—there were plenty of salmon in these rich waters. The market for the fish is what pitched Otto versus Sven in competition. The summer was one thing. But now in the off-season, when it was just the locals to feed, getting the catch to market first was crucial. There was nothing worse than getting to the grocer with your catch and being turned away because another fisherman got there first. Depending on the day, such a thing could make or break a pocketbook.

Sven was rumored to be about a hundred years old, but he was practiced and wily. His white hair sprouted out from his head like he was electrified and his eyes were the strangest shade of milky blue. Sven was prone to making nonsensical threats of sorcery and doom, and most Starfish Cove residents stayed out of his way.

Otto was glad to not spy his rival this morning. He reached the dock and made his way down the slippery wooden boards, holding the buckets outstretched in each arm for balance. To the right, something caught his eye—a flash of color from the pools caught in the rocky shelf that stretched between the docks and the cliffs.

He reversed his steps and hopped off of the ramp to investigate.

"Oh, matey," Otto muttered.

A large starfish with the most interesting appearance rested in a small, still pool. The animal was a robust salmon-orange in color, but its center was an iridescent blue, pulsing delicately like a strange, glowing heart.

Otto stepped onto a slick black rock and reached for the starfish. His fingers touched the sea animal and a small charge coursed up his arm. He jerked his hand away. He regarded the animal for a moment longer as the blue glow continued to throb in the starfish's center.

Otto turned abruptly and returned to the ramp. He shouldn't have gotten distracted—he had fishing to do. As he swung aboard, a sudden gust of wind made the boat rock from side to side.

Otto stumbled clumsily. A flash of irritation shot through him as he fired up Charlotte's motor. He'd been wasting the morning gaping at a starfish when he knew better than anyone that the weather could change faster than a rich lady changes dresses, not to mention that Sven had probably hauled his ancient self out of bed by now and was right on Otto's heels.

Otto motored out of the perfect half-moon of Starfish Cove, his eyes to the sky as dark clouds collected overhead. Otto pressed on, determined to get to the fishing waters before old Sven, at least for a few hours, weather be damned.

Rain began to fall, lightly at first, but then mounting quickly to fat drops that smacked heavily onto Otto's head. He swiped water from his eyes and pushed forward, even as beneath his feet came the familiar surge of an ocean growing angry. With each wave, the sea pushed his boat high towards the clouds and then sucked it down the backside of a wave.

Otto clung to the ship's wheel and rode the colossal waves, up, down, as he struggled to see into a sky that had become dark as night. He glimpsed a wave growing, the sea rising up and up, higher than he'd ever seen a wave rise before. Otto stared, terrified, as the massive wave lifted, lifted overhead. His boat hovered vulnerably in the trough as the wave continued to grow.

There was nowhere for Otto to go.

"Marion," he cried, uttering his wife's name for the last time.

A great wall of sea fell, crashing upon Otto and his boat in a cataclysmic wallop of destruction.

When the waters calmed, the surface of the sea revealed nothing but the gentle froth of the surf and the reflection of the sun shining brightly in the clear, blue sky.

TUESDAY, JANUARY 5, 1999

3:01 P.M.

The thunderstorm hovered offshore all day. Through English and P.E., a lunch of soggy fish sticks and tater tots, and then exhausting math and history, Skye kept her eyes to the west. The atmosphere was dark and shifted with boiling clouds. No lightning appeared, but the sky sparked as if any moment it would again unleash its fury.

After school, the rain fell hard. Skye pulled her hood over her head and stepped into the soggy parking lot, scanning for her brother. How was it that she hadn't seen him all day? She wanted to ask him what he'd seen this morning, and to fill him in on the return of the mom-darkness.

With her hand angled over her eyes, she searched for his 1979 Honda. Her hair whipped into her face until she scraped it back in a ponytail and tucked it into her jacket. Students slapped through ankle-deep puddles and held notebooks over their heads. Just because you lived on the Oregon Coast and knew rain was always possible didn't mean you dressed for it. Wet and stormy was as common as milk and cheerios—why get worked up about it? Boys in sneakers and girls in cute little flats waded across the flooding pavement like ill-prepared ducks. Skye hadn't done much better in her Converse, but at least she had worn socks and her jacket had a hood.

No Andrew. Ashley vanished after last period, too, mumbling something about going to the TV station. Skye didn't know what to do. She was so unsettled. She was only getting wet standing here. She should walk home. But instead her feet descended the stairs and began propelling her toward the dune. *It's dumb to go to the beach right now. It's so stormy.* But the ocean pulled her forward. *Just for a minute. Just to feel it out there.*

Skye struggled through wet sand to where the wind grew stronger and she could hear the crashing of the surf, and then she could see the sea, churning white and frothy huge. The power of the storm surged up the beach and pushed into her, and she anchored her feet to stay steady. Skye regarded the black clouds and the silvery surf and smiled despite the craziness. This much energy—it filled her up with excitement, like her own personal inner light.

One more breath and Skye whirled around and ran back down the dune. But instead of heading home, she turned south and padded down Coast Street one block to the narrow service road that climbed the cliff to the golf course.

Long ago, wealthy travelers came to Starfish Cove for the grand hotel on the north cliffs and the nine-hole golf course on the south cliffs. But the hotel had burned down decades ago and now the golf course was the only tourist destination left in town, unless you counted the tiny old aquarium on Main Street. Skye's father was the head groundskeeper, a job he liked for being outside with the forest and the ocean. But he had been tending grass for two decades now, battling the unwieldy weather and the wild coastal foliage, which had a tendency to grow like it was fed a potion out of a superhero movie. Skye thought he would happily walk away tomorrow, except for the paycheck—and her mother, who had no stomach for change.

Skye ran up the hill through fat raindrops. Water had made its way down the back of her neck and drenched the fabric of her blue jeans below the hem of her jacket. Panting and soaked, Skye crossed the last stretch of sodden ground and burst through the door of the doublewide trailer that served as golf course maintenance headquarters. On another day, she'd have found her dad running a ride-atop mower or chopping away at an errant salal, but today was a day for paperwork.

David's head popped up when she entered. "Stormy Skye!" he greeted her with a smile. "This sure is your kind of day, kiddo."

"Hey, Pops," she said, happy to see him but realizing she didn't really know why she'd come.

"Nice to see you here. What's up?" he asked, adding, "You're drenched."

He threw her one of the golf towels from the utility shelf behind his desk as she sank into an old wooden captain's chair. Skye ran the towel across her face and considered what she wanted to say.

"So," she said, studying her father's face. "Mom."

The two words were enough. Her dad folded his hands on the desk and returned her gaze with his thoughtful blue eyes. His brown curly hair was rumpled, as if he'd been kneading his head with his hands as he'd worked. After a moment, he nodded once.

"She was crying when I came home yesterday," Skye said. "The curtains were drawn."

"She's having a rough time right now," David acknowledged.

"I just wanted things to be different this year."

"I know. Me too."

"I don't know what to do when she's sad."

"We have to be patient and love her. She'll pull through."

Skye knew that was true. Her mother could be cheerful and loving, other times of the year. "I know," Skye said. "But not until after…" She trailed off, feeling guilty for even saying that much.

"Your birthday," David finished.

Skye lowered her eyes. The rain pounded on the trailer roof, filling the space between their words with a tinny drumming.

"It's lousy timing," David said. "Always has been."

Skye stared at her lap but gave a tiny nod. She loved having her father to herself. Away from her mom, he gave her his attention. He understood how she felt. Last year, her mom had tried to get it together for Skye's birthday. A few days before, Veronica brought home the candles and the cake ingredients—lemon cake with chocolate frosting,

Skye's favorite. But when Skye got home from school on her birthday, the cake mix was unopened on the counter and her mom was in bed.

It was her dad who went to the market and picked out a cake. It was all that they had left, a Winnie the Pooh cake, too babyish, and plain vanilla. But Skye blew out the candles and ate a piece anyway, after Andrew sang "Happy Birthday" off-key at the top of his lungs and her dad made rambunctious Tigger imitations. She was grateful for her dad and her brother. They always could make her laugh, even about the hard bad stuff.

Skye wound the damp cloth in her hands from end to end into a tight spiral, and then looked up at her dad. "Will you tell me the story again?"

Her dad didn't hesitate. He knew what she meant. "You were born on January 12, 1985. The day was a little bit like today."

Skye soaked up his words. She knew the story front to back, but hearing it was like a balm. It was a window into a time she didn't remember but desperately wanted to understand.

"The storms had been raging for nearly a week. They were some of the biggest storms on record for the Oregon Coast, and they were right here in Starfish Cove. Creeks turned to rivers, bridges were submerged, and roads were buried in landslides. Typhoon-strength winds knocked down dozens of trees."

Her father leaned into the story, laying on the drama. "Your mother and I made our way to the hospital under a wild sky. Your mom said the storm's power distracted her during the long hours of labor, nature's fury urging her on until your birth. The sky couldn't be escaped or ignored that day. So that's what we named you—Skye."

"And you added Stormy," Skye said, smiling.

David grinned. "It was my inside joke. The skies were stormy, but you were the most peaceful baby. Stormy stuck."

Skye tried to imagine storms so wild, her parents treasuring her arrival, and her mother happy. "Then what happened," she said. Her words came out as a statement rather than a question, because Skye knew the end of the story as well as the beginning.

"The weather continued," said David. "It worsened, in fact. For another three days."

"And on the last day of the storm..."

"...Your Aunt Penelope was gone." David placed his palms down on the desk to conclude the conversation.

But Skye wasn't finished. "And Mom has never been the same."

"And your mom has never been the same." Her dad had dropped the narrator tone, and his voice was tight and sad. "It was just too much for her, Stormy. That's the only way I can understand it. After her mother...and then her grandfather...it was just too much."

Skye looked away. On the wall hung a calendar with a photo of a golfer, mid-swing. "January" was printed in bold letters, as if to remind her what they were in the middle of. This morning's lightning and rain flashed in her mind, the way it came out of nowhere and chased her home. Her stomach clenched. She hadn't told anyone about being on the beach this morning. It felt safer to keep that to herself.

"We'll make your birthday nice, Stormy," David said gently. "I promise."

A gust of wind screamed over the top of the trailer. Rain splattered at the windows like machine gun fire and a clap of thunder shook the flimsy walls. A chill shot through Skye's body. The light bulb over David's desk flickered as the trailer leaned on its foundation, and then the lights went out.

"Let's get out of here," said her dad. "I've had enough for today."

TUESDAY, JANUARY 5, 1999

5:01 P.M.

Dark came early in the winter. Earlier still if it was stormy, and darker still if the power was out. Sheets of rain vanished into the gloom as the sun set over the sea. David drove the old Ford down the cliff to the streets of downtown past unlit houses. Rain slapped against the windows and wind shrieked over the cab. The heater fan hummed on high but struggled to deliver much warmth, and Skye shivered on the cold leather seat.

She thought about what her dad had said. Her mother never spoke a word about her sister, or any of the other members of her family. Even this time of year when losing Penelope was the only thing on Veronica's mind, her mother refused to discuss the past.

Skye had picked up a few pieces of information over the years, mostly from Andrew. Veronica and Penelope's mother had died when they were very young, but he didn't know how. The sisters had been raised by their grandfather, whose name was Wolfie. His wife was dead. Then Penelope died. Then Wolfie died. And Veronica didn't have any family left after that. Unless you counted David, Andrew and Skye. But somehow the dead seemed to take up more space than the living. Andrew called them The Dead Beckendorfs, as if they were a collective entity, a ghostly phenomenon with mysterious powers that overpowered everything else.

Why didn't Mom get out of bed today? Why is Mom crying in the garden? Why does it take Mom a hundred years to notice that I asked her a question? "The Dead Beckendorfs," Andrew would reply in his drama-voice, sweeping his hands through the air. Skye cringed at his dark humor, but he made her laugh.

Andrew told her that one had to laugh about this stuff; otherwise, it would just be massively sad. Still, Andrew never talked about The Dead Beckendorfs in front of their parents. He wasn't dumb.

The windshield wipers slapped violently from side to side and water collected across the road surface in a slick shimmering sheet. Most of the storefronts on Main Street were darkened, but ahead, on the right, was a golden glow. Her dad coasted to a stop at the curb. "Looks like Bob is staying open," he said. "Let's see how he's doing."

The Happy Oyster Bistro sat in the middle of the block, a few doors down from the aquarium. Skye's dad's friend Bob was the bistro's owner. His family had cultivated oyster beds for several decades. Before that, they'd been fishermen, but these days the fish were scarce and rules about catching them weren't. This year, Bob opened a seafood restaurant in the old Chowder Bowl location. Skye's dad snuck down here to help Bob out some evenings, when he could get away.

David hopped out of the truck and Skye followed, scurrying through the wind and rain to burst into the warm room, decorated with nets and floats, beach photos, and lots of objects featuring seagulls and lighthouses.

"Clancys!" Bob greeted them. He placed his hand on Skye's damp head, like she was a little girl. "Sit down! Have dinner."

"We probably should be getting home," said David. "Just wanted to check and see if you were okay here."

"Backup generators," winked Bob. "They've been saving our bacon. And our fish."

"Have you seen Andrew?" Skye asked Bob. Her brother had started working as dishwasher and busboy at the Oyster, to earn money for gas and insurance for his car.

"He's not on the schedule tonight," Bob replied, adding, "Why, is he missing?"

Skye forced a smile and kept her mouth shut. She probably missed her brother in the halls of Starfish Cove High today, and he was likely plopped on their couch at home right now, doing exactly nothing, and definitely not missing.

She checked her dad for a response, but he was staring at the flip-phone in his hand. He snapped it shut. "We've got to go."

"Take chowder," Bob said, disappearing into the kitchen and returning with a big paper bag before David could protest.

The phone beeped again and a dark look crossed David's face as he turned for the door. Skye trailed him.

"What's up?" she asked, after they'd buckled into the truck.

"Your mom's alone," he said. "The storm is scaring her. Let's roll."

A hitch caught in Skye's belly. *I guess that means Andrew isn't home.*

As they approached Coast and Main, Skye's father slowed, peering ahead to see if the streetlight was working. A bolt of lightning shot from the sky and a tremendous crack of thunder split the air. The flash lit up the intersection long enough to illuminate an object hurtling through the air right in front of the windshield.

Her dad slammed on the brakes to avoid colliding with whatever was swinging through the night. He leaned forward cautiously, his eyes searching the darkness. Every inch of Skye's skin began to tingle. The wipers swept a swath of water from the windshield and the object swung back the other way in a wild arc.

"The traffic light," her dad said, and Skye understood. The lightning bolt had knocked the old box-style traffic light loose from the cables and now it swung like a maniacal pendulum.

Another swipe of the wipers. Another glimpse of the light box sliding through the night sky like a surreal UFO. Before Skye could react, her father pushed open the truck door and leapt into the darkness.

TUESDAY, JANUARY 5, 1999
5:29 P.M.

"Dad!" Skye called, but her father was gone. She peered through the windshield, searching for her father in the dark and stormy outside. The traffic light swung again, a black menacing mass twisting in the wind. Rain smeared across the windshield, hampering her vision.

Skye caught a flash of movement and a figure flitted around the side of the truck towards the intersection. Her father carried something in each hand, a stick of some kind. Skye's heart slammed in her chest and her skin was hot and prickly. She wanted to jump out of the truck after him, but fear kept her pinned to her seat.

Her father vanished and appeared; he vanished and appeared in the muted path of the headlights. Another flash of lightning brought the whole scene to a shocking glow for an instant, her father and the light box lit up, eerie and blinding.

Her father lifted both sticks in the air and swept them together in front of him, capturing the cable above the light box. He walked awkwardly to the right, disappearing

31

from view again. She squinted as hard as she could, but she couldn't see anything through the steady rainfall. A minute passed. Another. Skye's breath came fast. Should she get out of the truck? The truck door flew open and her father climbed inside, his face red and his breath heavy. Skye reached for his arm—his canvas jacket was soaked with rain and clammy cold.

"What the heck, dad," she managed. "Are you trying to die?"

David let out a low, stilted chortle. "Yeah," he said under his breath. "I mean, no," he turned to her. "I was never going to die."

"What were those things?" Skye said.

"Golf clubs," David replied. "Rubber handles. Anti-current. I pulled the light box to the pole and secured it until someone can fix it. We'll call the city when we get home."

Skye didn't say anything. Images of the swinging light and the fuzzy figure of her father darting through the storm floated before her eyes.

"We've got to get home," David said, turning the key to bring the truck's engine to life with a low growl.

Skye and her dad rolled into the driveway as another flash of lightning pierced the sky. The blinds were drawn and the house was dark. She grabbed her backpack and sprinted for the door through muddy puddles. Skye burst in, scanning the room. Her mother huddled at one end of the couch, as she had the day before. An emergency lantern glowed from the side table. Leopold the cat slept beside her.

David stood behind Skye in the doorway. "We stopped to check on Bob," he said. It went without saying that the traffic light situation would not be mentioned.

Veronica nodded slightly. She looked more stunned than sad, as if the weather and power outage had shut her down completely.

"We brought chowder," David offered, shrugging off his drenched jacket and hanging it by the door. Skye kicked her soaked Converse to the floor and sat by her mother, reaching for her hand. "Are you hungry?" David asked.

Veronica shook her head no. Her dark curls fell around her face, hiding her features. Skye tried to think of something to say. *Everything's going to be okay, Mom. It's just a storm. No one is going to die.* The words all sounded lame in her head. How could she promise her mother that no one would die in a storm when all Veronica could think of was that someone had died in a storm? This was the worst part of the mom-darkness, feeling so helpless.

The lamp flickered back to life and the VCR clock started blinking red. Veronica startled at the sudden light, rising awkwardly to amble down the hall. David followed.

Skye was alone. She tugged her hoodie zipper up and down a few times to hear the metallic zing of the teeth. Her mother's sadness seemed heavier this year. Maybe Skye was just hyper-aware of it. Today's storm certainly wasn't helping.

Skye reached for the remote and flipped on the television. Jerry Petrichor appeared on screen, his blue dress shirt and purple tie a bit disheveled, his face as handsome as ever. "Good evening, Starfish Cove! And compliments to the power company for excellent timing in getting us back up and running. Welcome to our 7 p.m. news and weather segment. Thunderstorms continue and a traffic light is out downtown, on this, the evening of one of the most epic weather days in a long time."

Skye pulled a crocheted blanket over her lap as Jerry continued. "High wind gusts of up to 65 miles per hour were reported on the bluffs today, and we've accumulated 2.8 inches of rain so far today." Footage played of the thunderstorm hanging offshore. "Here at KTSC, today's wild weather has been bringing back memories of the storms of 1985, which occurred almost exactly 14 years ago. As many of you recall, extreme weather struck our coastline for two solid weeks, causing incredible damage to the infrastructure of our fair city and tragically claiming one Starfish Cove resident."

Skye blew out a quick breath, glad her mother wasn't in the room for this one.

"There's no reason to believe that this weather will continue or reach the heights that it did 14 years ago. The forecast looks relatively calm." Jerry paused, looking directly into the camera. "However, curiously, the forecast this morning didn't predict the disturbance we received."

He gestured at the weather map, where bold colors hovered over Starfish Cove. "Furthermore, you can see here that the current storm is localized, centered right over our little town. Our coastal neighbors are experiencing much milder weather."

Jerry filled the screen again. "Which makes me wonder—what makes us so special? Tune in tomorrow to learn what's in store for us next."

Skye clicked the television off, thinking. Today's storm hadn't turned up in the forecasting systems. The weather was the worst here. Skye tipped her head back and closed her eyes. Her head churned with images—lightning striking the beach, moody black clouds, the swinging traffic light, her mother's face.

And where the heck was her brother?

Skye retrieved the forgotten bag of chowder from the bench by the front door. She spooned lukewarm soup into her mouth as she did her homework at the kitchen table, and then crawled into bed early, to the ominous sounds of offshore thunder and a relentless, driving rain.

WEDNESDAY, JANUARY 6, 1999

7:41 A.M.

Skye awoke to thunder. Rain hit her window in a steady patter. The remnants of a dream lingered. The churning sea. A white-tipped mountain. A pulsing blue light. Murky clouds zooming across a starlit sky. She grasped to remember more but all was slipping away.

"Stormy!" Her eyes flew open and the last bits of the dream fled from her mind. "Get up! I lost my ceee-real."

Andrew, yelling at the top of his lungs outside of her door. Skye took a deep breath but didn't respond. Apparently, Andrew forgot that he ate all of his cereal two days ago.

"Stormy!" Andrew hollered. "I know you're hoarding it in there. Mom and Dad are gone already. We have to leave for school soon, and I'm hangry."

Skye bristled, caught between relief and annoyance. She'd been wondering where her brother was and now he was back in full, irritating glory. Why on earth would she be keeping cereal in her room? That was ridiculous.

"Andrew!" she barked. "I didn't take your stupid Sugar

Flakes! You ate them!"

She hauled herself out of bed and pulled on a hoodie over her pajamas. The air was damp and clammy. She wished she could slide back under the covers and spend the day watching *Brady Bunch* reruns.

"Stooormmmeeey!" Andrew howled.

Skye shoved her feet into her bunny slippers and jerked open the door, prepared to wage war. Andrew grinned and leapt up and down in the hall, holding a box of Sugar Flakes in both hands like a giddy toddler.

"Gotcha!" he said.

Skye was about to slam her door shut on his gleeful face, but she couldn't help it: she smiled. Andrew was such a weirdo goofball sometimes.

"Want cereal?" he asked, pogo-sticking in the hall, his curly brown hair flopping. "Dad bought me more."

"You know sugar makes me feel like a dead walrus, Andrew," Skye said, pushing past him and ambling down the hall.

"That's weird. And too bad for you, bro." Andrew followed her, giving the cereal box a hug.

"Where were you yesterday?" Skye demanded. "I didn't see you all day—I started to think you were dead. And where were you last night? I could've used some company."

"Well, Stormy," Andrew said in a low theatrical voice. "That's a story for another time."

"Whatever," Skye said, shuffling into the kitchen. The room was empty except for the cat. The curtains were open to a soggy, grey world. Raindrops flew at the window, and

37

the rhododendron lashed back and forth as if someone was shaking it.

"Hi, Leopold," Skye murmured, turning away from the gloomy view and giving the cat a rub on the head as he ate from a bowl on the floor.

"Meow," said Leopold, through a mouthful of chicken bits and gravy.

"The cat says 'meow,'" said Andrew as he dumped half of the box of cereal into a mixing bowl.

Skye retrieved the eggs from the fridge and cracked a few in a pan, navigating a slurry of emotion. She was grateful to see her brother, but she'd hoped she'd wake to calmer skies this morning—that the weather would improve and her mother would feel less frightened and everything would be better somehow.

"Did you see Mom and Dad this morning?" she asked.

"Briefly," he said, munching cereal and staring at the cat.

Skye scooped eggs onto her plate and added a dash of pepper. "How were they?"

"They seemed okay."

Skye nodded noncommittally.

"What's up?" asked Andrew.

Skye leaned up against the countertop and tried to steady her voice. "Mom," she said. "You know."

Andrew nodded and rolled his eyes. "I guess that was to be expected."

"Yeah," Skye said. "It still sucks."

"Yup," said Andrew, scooping the last bite into his mouth. "It'll pass. You know it always does."

An aching hollow pulled at Skye's belly. "But isn't there anything we can do?"

Andrew shrugged. "In my personal past experience," he said, "I'd say that's a no."

"There's got to be something," Skye said testily.

Andrew sighed and plunked his bowl into the sink, causing the cat to flee the kitchen. "Here's how it goes, Stormy," he began. "Every January, Mom gets sad. Really, *really* sad. Like the memory of The Dead Beckendorfs is on a time clock burned into her body to go off at this exact time of year. She seizes up and disappears and cries and whatever, and then as soon as the date Penelope died passes, she's fine again. Like the whole thing has to run her over again every single year. And we can't do anything about it."

Skye regarded her brother. "You sound annoyed," she said, putting her uneaten eggs on the counter behind her.

"Well, it's kind of annoying! I mean, it's super crappy that her sister died, and her mother and grandfather and all of the rest of them, but shouldn't she be over it by now?"

Skye waited a few beats to see if Andrew would answer his own question. He looked at his sister defiantly, waiting for her to challenge him. A gust of wind screamed by the window outside, throwing water up against the glass with a sharp splatter.

"I don't know," said Skye. "Should she be over it?"

Andrew released his breath noisily. "I don't know. Apparently not. It just seems so…self-destructive. I mean, why are we still even *in* this town? In this *house*, even? Where everything reminds Mom of The Dead Beckendorfs."

Skye sighed. "I don't know. Dad says Mom is afraid to leave."

Andrew rolled his eyes again. "Yeah, because staying is working out so well. Anyway," he continued, "she went to work with Dad this morning. So maybe that will cheer her up or at least distract her for a while. Better than sitting here with the curtains drawn."

"That's good." Skye felt lighter.

Andrew glanced at the microwave clock. "We have to roll." Skye had lost track of time. She looked down at her feet in her bunny slippers and hurried off to change for school.

Five minutes later, the Clancy siblings had stomped across the soggy lawn and were motoring through the flooded abyss of Clark Street in Andrew's Honda. The sky was thick with clouds and spat dense droplets onto the windshield.

The Honda had been their dad's. When Andrew turned 16 a few months ago, David unearthed the car from the garage. Despite the years, the car was in decent shape, and Andrew treated it like an old, gentle pet—delicately, and with love. The car had a vintage tape deck and Andrew was now in possession of a small collection of David's 80s cassettes. He popped in Depeche Mode and navigated cavernous potholes. "Seeing that storm from the band room yesterday morning was insane," he said.

"Ah!" pounced Skye. "Band, yesterday morning? So all I need of the 'story for another time' is where you were last night."

Andrew twisted his lips. "Well, last night, I was getting

dumped. Spectacularly, fantastically dumped."

Skye pictured Lucy and her pretty face that was usually made un-pretty because she scrunched it up in irritation. "You're too good for her," Skye said.

Andrew shrugged. At the intersection at Coast and Main, temporary stop signs were set up at all four corners. The stoplight was still attached to the pole where her dad had secured it. Andrew studied the scene. She considered filling him in, but the nervous feeling in her belly stopped her.

She peered into the boiling sky thought about her mother. How could she have forgotten to watch Jerry this morning? She needed to know what the weather was going to do today. She didn't agree with Andrew. Veronica should have stayed home. There was nothing good about her being up on that cliff with the dank sky swirling over her head.

"Andrew," she blurted. "Sneak out with me at lunch. I want to go to the golf course and check on Mom and Dad."

MAY 24, 1920

ALICE BECKENDORF

Alice climbed the cliff trail and thought about love. When she was little, she believed by the age of 19 she'd have found a fellow. *How foolish to have been certain of such a thing,* she thought as she made her way up the high bluff to the fancy hotel. Finding a match was much more difficult than she'd ever known, especially when one was confined to a tiny oceanfront town in Oregon.

Alice pushed her woeful love life out of her mind and took in the expansive view. She adored this stretch of seascape—the wind rising from the sea to ruffle the salal plants, the crashing surf below, the charming sight of the hotel and its wealthy guests ahead.

Every day after her job at the grocer, Alice walked here. Today, the day was pleasantly warm and the Pacific aglow with sunshine, though a strong breeze tugged at the lengths of Alice's long skirts, which whipped around her favorite high-buttoned black boots. Her hair was pulled into a secure bun, but the wind pulled strands free to brush against her cheeks.

Here she was, a grown woman, gainfully employed, free to buy her own lunches and dresses and sweets. Yet she lived with her mother in a drab little cottage. And worse, the suitors to choose from were the very same boys she'd always known, who'd pulled at her braids and called her Curly, for her long spiral curls. Like Donald, whose boyhood pestering had recently evolved into adoration that she only wished she could possibly return. Donald asked her to accompany him to every social occasion the town produced, from dances at the grange to crab feeds at the shore.

But alas, Alice only had eyes for Frank—Frank of the wavy blond hair and the strong chin, Frank of the wool suits and the charming smile, Frank whose family had owned the mercantile since before they were both born. Now she worked beside him five days a week, and yet he barely looked at her.

Perhaps her fate with suitors would have been different if she'd had a father. It was a pointless thing to ponder. No logic in wishing for that which never had been. Her father Otto was a fisherman who had been lost at sea before she was born. Her mother, Marion, had brought up Alice and her big brother, Wolfie, on her own. Now Wolfie was away at Normal School studying to become a schoolteacher, so she didn't even have him to lean on.

Alice caught her toe on a shore pine root and caught herself from falling. The Hotel Starfish Cove was before her. Alice took in the grand wood and stone structure with the gabled roof and the spacious wraparound deck. An American flag bigger than she'd seen anywhere else flew from a pole out front.

It was early in the season—the majority of the guests wouldn't arrive for a month or more. But a smattering of people reclined in marvelous rocking chairs overlooking the ocean. Alice daydreamed about one day sitting there herself, lounging in the summer breeze. Her Uncle Bertram worked as the caretaker here, and lived in a small cabin tucked into the woods behind the hotel. Alice envied his position, even if he was just the help.

Alice strode determinedly a bit further before turning on her heel and returning the way she'd come. She'd walked this trail so many times before that she could travel in a contented daze, and now found herself nearing the descent to the cove once more. She made her way down, picking her way through the rocky section at the top to wind into the woods for a stretch before the trail turned back to the sandy beach and the tide pools.

Alice liked to end her day's walk here, picking her way over the glistening rust-colored rocks to peer into the tide pools and search for small animals—purple urchin, green anemone, starfish, and especially the small crab that camouflaged so well against the rocks.

As Alice approached the pools, something caught her eye. She could have sworn she'd seen a blue flash from a pool. She quickened her pace over the slippery rocks—yes, there it was again. A pulse of blue light. Alice reached the pool and saw a starfish, quite large. Astonishingly, the light seemed to be coming from the animal's middle.

How curious. She bent for a closer look. The echinoderm itself was plump and looked completely normal, except its interior glowed a fantastic blue at regular intervals. After a period of observation, Alice reached gingerly into shallow water. At the moment of contact, energy transferred from the starfish's skin into her own fingers. "My," she breathed. "You are a lovely creature."

Alice crouched on a rock and pondered the amazing sight. A gust blasted off the water, colder on her skin than the day's air had been thus far. "My," she said again, this time in surprise at the wind's sudden frosty nature. She rose and turned to make her way home and quite unexpectedly encountered the icy prick of precipitation stinging her face. Without warning, massive clouds filled the sky and sleet peppered her skin.

Alice pulled her spring sweater around her body. She made haste across the sand only to witness the sleet turn to snow before her eyes. Snow in May on the Oregon Coast! Unheard of. Alice gazed about in shock as the snowflakes fell heavier and thicker by the moment. She tried to push on but she was surrounded in a curtain of white. Alice was utterly unsure which way was which. At her feet, snow accumulated rapidly, covering her boots to the ankle.

"Wolfie!" she cried out, wishing against all reason that her brother would somehow hear her call for help.

But there was no reply except for the wind and the snow, which whispered Alice's name, calling to her until she believed that relenting to their icy invitation was what she was meant to do all along.

10

WEDNESDAY, JANUARY 6, 1999

8:45 A.M.

The halls of Starfish Cove High School were steamy and smelled like wet shoes. Students shook out raincoats, fluffed damp hairdos and attempted to dry moist pieces of homework against ancient oil-powered wall heaters.

Skye found Ashley leaning against the locker they shared. She had a crumbling blueberry muffin in one hand and her dripping backpack in the other. "Need help with the combo?" Skye asked, giving her friend a side-hug.

"Sure," said Ashley, curling into a shrug. "I was totally going to remember it in a minute."

"I'm here for you, Quick." It was ironic that Ashley's last name was Quick, the same way that Skye's moody mother should have been called Stormy instead of even-keeled Skye. But especially this morning with so much on her mind, Skye envied the way Ashley meandered unworried through life. Skye overthought everything, digging into worries and dwelling there like a mole in a dark hole. That was definitely not Ashley's condition.

"Where did you go yesterday after school?" asked

46

Skye, after she'd cracked the code on their locker and opened its creaky metal door.

"TV station," Ashley replied. "My mom was worried because of the weird weather and didn't want me out on the loose."

"I still can't believe your mom gets to work with Jerry Petrichor every day."

"He's not that big of a deal, Skye. You can come and meet him anytime. He's just a person."

"No, no, no. Nope."

"How are you going to be a weather reporter if you're afraid to talk to one?"

Skye shrugged. "I'm not sure. I haven't figured that out."

"Right," replied Ashley, twirling a pretend mustache and donning an English accent. "Excellent plan."

"Did you watch the weather this morning?" Skye asked. Maybe Ashley could fill her in on what she'd missed.

"Nope," said Ashley. "I lived in it, though." She looked at her squishy pink and purple Vans.

The five-minute warning bell sounded and Ashley grabbed her notebook, calling "Toodles!" as she sashayed away.

Skye suffered through the morning as rain and wind whipped the school. The storm didn't seem to be letting up at all. The bell for lunch period rang, and Skye rose with her classmates and filed out of the classroom.

She was nervous about what they, she and Andrew, were about to do. Leaving school during the day was a no-go, even at lunchtime. In the hall, Skye rose on her tiptoes and caught a glimpse of her brother up ahead. She pushed past kids to scurry forward. "Andrew!" she called, slinking around a couple holding hands and pushing past a group of blonds in short skirts.

"Hey, Stormy," he said. "Ready for the party?"

"What party?" she replied automatically. Her mind was skittery.

"Your birthday party." He raised his arms in the air and did a little shimmy with his hips.

"It's not my birthday for six days," Skye hissed. "Are we going to do this or not?"

"Always so serious, bro. But yes, of course we are."

They entered the crowded cafeteria, bypassing hot lunch lines and tables full of kids to make their way to the back of the room, where doors exited to the parking lot. They were just about to slide out the door when Mr. Terwilliger, the PE teacher, appeared out of nowhere.

"Hello, Clancys," he said. "Where are you off to?"

"She has to go to the bathroom," Andrew said, pointing at Skye.

"He does, too." Skye shot her brother a sharp look. Her heart was hammering in her chest.

"Are you serving as each other's interpreter?" asked Mr. Terwilliger.

"Yes," Andrew and Skye declared together.

"In that case, perhaps you can inform each other that the restroom is not in the parking lot."

"Right," said Skye.

"Knew that," said Andrew.

"Try the hall," added Mr. Terwilliger.

48

Skye followed her brother as he skirted the room, dodging kids and moving quickly. Skye glanced back over her shoulder; Mr. Terwilliger followed their retreat with suspicious eyes.

They hit a quick jog down the hall and blasted through the door at the end of the hall before they could change their minds. Exhilaration dissolved to dread at the sight of the sky. Dark clouds billowed overhead, moving across the sky at a fearsome pace. The clouds were alive with a murky force as flashes of electrical energy sparked in charcoal centers.

Andrew looked towards the school. They couldn't go back—someone would surely see them return. And getting the Honda would take too much time and attract attention. He grabbed Skye by the arm and the two set out in a run under a sky that boiled dark and grey like campfire smoke.

WEDNESDAY, JANUARY 6, 1999

12:20 P.M.

Skye and Andrew pounded down the slick street. The roiling clouds cast a spooky light on the rickety beach houses of Pacific Street. They pushed up the hill as the sky crackled overhead. The humidity and electricity had done amazing things to Andrew's hair, which sprouted in damp spikes off of the top of his head. In his blue jeans and polo shirt, and with that hair and his soaking wet loafers, he looked like a cross between a Land's End catalog model and a mad scientist.

Skye's mind was a muddle. Events of the last two days swam together, impossibly intertwined. The weather. Her mother's state of mind. The anniversary of the storms. Her strange dream. It all seemed a messy whole, something she couldn't see completely but couldn't pull apart either.

They crested the hill and approached the golf course. The sky growled and spat a drizzle upon them. Skye felt the clouds watching them, waiting until she and Andrew were exposed before they would unleash a powerful vengeance.

That's ridiculous. Clouds weren't evil protagonists who

could make decisions about who to harm. *The weather isn't personal.*

Still, on top of a hill was the worst possible place to be during a storm. Skye was about to mention this when they reached the edge of the golf course. Ahead was the grand cedar clubhouse, Starfish Cove's most amazing structure, even at 50 years of age. The building was two elegant stories of wood and glass overlooking a sweeping view of the sea.

Hovering above it was a black, looming cloud. From the cloud's center descended a swirling tube.

Slivers of dread spread in Skye's body. The cylinder expanded and reached towards the clubhouse like a menacing hand. A howling screech cut through the air.

Skye dug her fingers into Andrew's arm as the branches of the shore pine overhead began to lash in the wind. The force pushed Andrew and Skye backwards and they clung to the lowest branches of the tree as the ground began to vibrate beneath their feet.

The tip of the whirlwind touched the north end of the clubhouse roof and shattered it. Shingles sucked into the vortex. Three windows exploded, tossing glittering shards of glass towards the green. Slabs of wood spun in the air, whirling around the tube until they were jettisoned out and hurtled to the earth. Just feet from where they stood, wood hit soil with powerful thumps and jammed black divots into the grass.

The last of the cedar shingles smacked to the earth. The whirlwind withdrew gracefully into the cloud. The screeching silenced and the wind ceased.

The world became eerily calm.

Skye's heart hammered and she refused to let go of the rough bark of the branch. The cloud glided towards the sea innocently, as if it had nothing to do with the disaster below on the ground. Sunrays appeared, illuminating the green with slices of light.

Andrew and Skye hunkered under the tree, taking in the damage. The green was strewn with debris. Splintered wood and glass surrounded the clubhouse, which was missing half of its roof.

"Wicked!" Andrew broke the silence, leaping in excitement. "That was awesome! Guess the clubhouse didn't need its roof anymore."

Skye didn't feel quite so giddy. She was dizzy and queasy. Watching a roof removed by a villainous cloud was surreal and yet familiar, way too similar to yesterday morning's lightning storm.

Where were her parents? She started towards the building but Andrew grabbed her hoodie, jerking her back under the tree.

"What the heck?" she complained, straightening her twisted sweatshirt. "We have to find Mom and Dad."

"Hold on," he whispered. "And be quiet!"

Andrew pointed towards the maintenance trailer. Their father stood on the stair outside the door, scanning the scene. Behind him, Veronica hovered in the doorway, her face pale and frightened.

"Mom and Dad are safe," Andrew hissed, pulling her behind a row of shrubbery. "And they'll kill us if they know we're here. Mom would keel over and die on the spot."

Across the green, Veronica clung to the stair rail, her body tense with fear and grief. Skye wanted to go to her, but she knew her brother was right. If Veronica knew they'd ditched school and had been exposed to that monster cloud, she'd freak out.

"We need to go back to school," Andrew said. "Like, now."

The two ran down the glistening road towards school as the sky opened bright and clear above them.

WEDNESDAY, JANUARY 6, 1999

1:45 P.M.

Skye and Andrew slunk back in the school's back door. Skye hoped they would be able to slip down the hall and into class undisturbed. Instead, there stood Mr. Terwilliger, leaning against a cinder block wall with his arms crossed.

"Clancys," he said. "How nice of you to grace us with your presence."

Andrew and Skye were cornered like mice in a trap.

"Gave us the slip, did you?" Mr. Terwilliger's voice was level, and Skye couldn't tell which direction this encounter would go. She fidgeted. Skye wasn't used to getting into trouble. She slid her brother a look.

"We checked on our parents," Andrew blurted. "Up at the golf course."

"I see. In a raging storm, you were worried about your parents, but not your own safety," replied Mr. Terwilliger. "Or the school rules."

"Yeah," said Andrew. "Something like that."

Mr. Terwilliger continued to stare them down, his arms

folded over his chest. He was a big man, older than their father by at least a decade. Skye had never thought that much about Mr. Terwilliger, and she figured he'd never thought about them much either. But his hazel eyes studied them now as if he was analyzing their entire destiny.

"All right," Mr. Terwilliger said, pushing away from the wall. "During your absence, classes resumed. Please return to 5th period. And *stay* there."

"Thanks," Andrew said gratefully. Skye was too flustered to speak and only nodded mutely. She and her brother skittered down the hall towards their lockers.

"Clancys," called Mr. Terwilliger after them. "One more thing. You especially should know to take caution with the weather of Starfish Cove."

"Okay, Mr. Terwilliger," Andrew said over his shoulder. "Thanks!"

"What does *that* mean?" Skye mumbled.

"I don't know. I can't believe he let us go."

Skye and Andrew reached the hallway split—Skye's locker was to the right, Andrew's to the left. Andrew turned to go. "See you, Stormy."

Skye's mind whirled: the roof whirling in the air, her mother cowering in the doorway. "Andrew, wait!"

Her brother returned to her side. He waited. But now she didn't know what to say. So many strange thoughts mashed up together. Nothing was clear but her dread. "Something's wrong," she managed.

Andrew's playful eyes were serious for once. "Yeah, Stormy," he responded. "The roof of the clubhouse just blew off before our very eyes. It's probably normal if you feel like something is wrong."

"No, I mean…it's bigger than that." The words came out in a jumble. "I had this dream. And I haven't even told you about the beach. Or the traffic light."

Andrew took her forearm. "Skye," he said. "The roof was old, and it was windy. Everything's okay. We need to get back to class. Let's talk about it after school."

Andrew gave her arm a squeeze and ambled down the hall. Skye watched him go and felt no relief from the pit of discomfort in her gut. Before she turned towards her locker, she looked down the hallway to the door that they had come in a few minutes before.

Mr. Terwilliger stood there, watching her.

AUGUST 12, 1945

BERTRAM BECKENDORF

Bertram was tired, and not just because he was 72 years old. He was tired of fighting for the fish in the sea off of Starfish Cove, tired of being treated like the town curmudgeon, tired of being alone, tired of people dying and tired of eating beans from the can for dinner. Mostly, he was tired of the weather. Right now, hunkered in his cabin on the north cliff, he was tired of being tired.

"Bah!" he said, rising from his worn rocker. It was time to shake off this terrible mood. Perhaps good old-fashioned fresh air would do the trick. He tugged his slicker from the nail and threw open the door. The sight was something to behold.

Raindrops flew sideways across the clearing between his cabin and the cliff front. Shore pine waved wildly in the wind like seasick sailors. Storm clouds fluffy as mashed potatoes surged through the sky overhead, delivering steady buckets of rain onto the churning sea below.

"Bah!" Bertram hollered, barreling through the door

like a 20-year-old soldier dead-set on battle instead of the tired old man he was.

The rain pounded his face and soaked his clothing, but succeeded in making Bertram feel alive. He'd grown up in Starfish Cove, fished its unruly waters, and lived in this rustic cabin during his time as caretaker of Hotel Starfish Cove and ever since the hotel burned down a decade ago. He'd faced adversity. But nothing had topped the last couple of weeks.

The weather had been so bad Bertram had begun to feel as if he was cursed. The roof had been torn from his shed by a wind gust, a tree had fallen on his old Ford and caved in the rear right end, his yard had flooded and sent water right under his front door into the kitchen, and his old trawler Nelly had been jerked here and there on her lashings at the dock until the sides had bashed in. Not since his brother Otto had been lost at sea and his niece had frozen to death twenty years later had Bertram been so angry at nature.

Bertram slammed his soggy boots across the sodden grass towards the cliff. He wanted to holler at the angry sky. *Unleash your fury on me! I can take it. I still have a fight left in me.* He marched right up to the edge of the cliff, wavering in the wind with his coattails flapping as he looked down below at the extraordinary sight.

After the hotel burned and the fish business suffered and the dock fell into disrepair, most of the other fishermen relocated their vessels to the new harbor at Chinook. But Bertram liked it here with a clear view of his boat below, even if most of the time he was alone in the woods. Only his brother's boy, Wolfie, paid him a visit occasionally. Wolfie and Bertram never had much in common. Wolfie wanted nothing of a life spent at sea or working the land. He'd become a teacher, and taught math and physical education at the high school, something Bertram couldn't relate to any more than he could flying to the moon.

"Bah!" Bertram spat out loud at the stormy sea, shaking his fists over his head. The thing was, Bertram did feel something strange in his tired old bones, a sense of dreadful energy following him around. And he knew when this unsettling feeling had begun, too. It was when he'd spotted that odd starfish weeks ago.

He'd been walking towards the docks from the base of the cliff on a perfectly lovely day, when out of the corner of his eye he spotted the most bizarre creature in the tide pools. On closer inspection, it appeared to be a perfectly normal starfish except for its center, which glowed blue. Pulsing iridescent cerulean blue, as if straight from outer space.

Bertram had taken a step back from the bizarre thing. He certainly hadn't touched it. He boarded Nelly, but curiosity had gotten the best of him and he'd returned to the tide pool, unsure whether his hope was to rescue the creature or put it out of its misery. But it was gone. The water lapped over the tide pool, splashing anemone and urchins, no starfish in sight.

The moment he reboarded Nelly, a stiff wind slid down the cove from the north, sending a chill to his core. He set out to sea as he had intended, but dark clouds gathered steadily, accumulating more quickly than he'd ever witnessed. Bertram peered into the gathering darkness and considered. He had spent enough days on the sea to develop a certain sixth sense about the elements, and now, all of his intuitive alarm bells were firing. Bertram made a decision—he would skip fishing today. He wheeled Nelly for shore, arriving at the dock as massive raindrops pelted him on the head.

A decision he didn't regret, and yet, a strange series of events had followed. He'd been haunted by wicked weather and bad luck ever since. When Wolfie called on him, Bertram told him about the strange starfish and the terrible things that had happened, and how it had made him wonder what had really happened to Otto, and even to Alice, but Wolfie completely dismissed Bertram's words as a nonsensical rant.

That was a few days ago, and things had only gotten worse. Bertram left his suspicions on the wall of his cabin, and that was all that he could do.

He was tired of it all so much. From the edge of the cliff, he confronted the cruel sky. Bertram stood at the precipice and hollered, "Give me all that you've got!"

As if in immediate answer, a marvelous bright bolt of lightning flew from a cloud in a vibrant crack, striking Bertram directly on top of the head. He never felt a thing, and fell peacefully to the ground in a heap.

WEDNESDAY, JANUARY 6, 1999
3:31 P.M.

After school, Skye went to the beach. She worked her way up the crest of the dune and tried to clear her mind. The fresh air and the sight of her favorite beach under a blue sky helped. Was it truly only yesterday morning that she'd walked right into that thunderstorm at dawn? The past day and a half felt like a hundred years.

Skye strode towards the waterline where sandpipers moved gracefully in gentle waves. She reached the surf and looked to the sea, rocking back and forth, thinking. She was less freaked out than earlier, but her thoughts still wouldn't settle. The weather was calm now, at least. Were the storms behind them?

"Hey." The voice came right behind her head, startling her from her thoughts. "You disappeared after school," said Andrew, adding, "I figured this is where I might find you."

A quick breeze caught at her hair and she re-secured her ponytail. "Yeah," she said. "I needed to think."

"So what's up?"

Skye considered what she wanted to say. "I knew Mom shouldn't have gone up there today," she began. "To the golf course. I had a bad feeling."

"You couldn't have known what was going to happen, Stormy."

"It's just...everything feels all mixed up together." The thoughts in her head began tying themselves into a muddle again. "Mom. The storms. January."

Andrew dug a toe into the sand, creating a divot that filled with water when he pulled his shoe back out. "I'm not following you."

"It seems like the mom-darkness is worse than ever before. And this weather is so..." she struggled for a word that wouldn't sound crazy. "Unusual. What if those things are connected?"

"How?" Andrew asked.

"I don't know," Skye admitted, gazing towards the Old Docks. She turned quickly back to Andrew, blurting what had crystalized in her mind. "What if all of Mom's worries about storms over the years actually made them happen? What if this year, the one thing she's feared the most, she created?"

Andrew cast his eyes upwards and took in a long breath. "Skye. Our mother may be a powerful worrier, but I'm pretty sure she can't control the weather."

Skye was about to agree with him when a blast of cold wind coursed off of the sea, pushing Skye and Andrew back onto their heels. The sandpipers took off at once in a noisy flutter. The sea whipped up before them, the next wave coming higher and faster at their feet. Caught off-guard, they backtracked in unison away from the incoming water.

Skye looked up, trying to make sense of the sudden change of events. The sky remained crystal clear as the wind continued to blast off the sea.

"Stormy! Let's go!"

Andrew was right beside her, but the wind pulled at his words and threw them into the sky. He turned her from the ocean, but the wind came from that direction too. It seemed to be circling wildly, coming at them from all angles.

The dune wasn't far, but suddenly it seemed like a mile away. The wind caught the dry sand at the top of the beach and whirled it into the air. Now they walked in a sandstorm, grains pelting their bodies. Skye tried to speak, but the wind pushed into her mouth, snuffed out the words. Andrew gestured ahead to the rise of the dune.

She leaned in, forcing her feet forward. Her hair came loose, and flew wildly as sand stung her face. Andrew's clothing flapped against his body and sand lifted off of the ground to circle around him as if he were the nexus of a tornado. The wind screeched in her ears, a high-pitched shriek like a thousand screams.

The Clancys fought their way over the hill and hurried to Andrew's Honda. Skye pulled on the door, holding tight to keep it from being torn from her grip. She fell into the passenger seat and slammed the door, reveling in the sudden safety and silence.

Andrew landed next to her in the driver's seat, pulling his door shut heavily. He took a few breaths, scraping his hand over his sand-covered face.

After a moment, he looked up calmly and said, "What were you saying, Stormy?"

The look on his face was mock-serious, as if they'd normally picked up their conversation from the beach. Skye laughed, a nervous giggle that came tumbling out unevenly, until the giggle morphed into a sob. She couldn't stop it—tears sprung from her eyes and rolled down her sandy cheeks.

Her chest heaved and she took a moment to gather herself. "I was saying—I think something's wrong."

Andrew's skin was ashen, and there was no humor in his voice this time. "Tell me about the traffic light."

Skye related the events of yesterday morning on the beach, and of last night, as the wind howled outside of the Honda, tugging at the beach grasses on the hill and pushing at the car like an angry animal trying to get in.

WEDNESDAY, JANUARY 6, 1999
4:36 P.M.

Skye and Andrew pulled into the driveway just after 4:30. Their parents would be waiting—Wednesdays, David worked as chef and Andrew as busser at the Happy Oyster, where they were due by 5.

Skye climbed out of the Honda, half-expecting to be blasted by a gust of wind, or possibly she and the whole house would simply lift to the sky like Dorothy in the *Wizard of Oz*. But Clark Street was calm, and her Converse stayed firmly planted to the earth.

She grabbed the front of her hoodie and shook it, watching sand rain steadily to the ground. Andrew bent to one side and rubbed his scalp vigorously, loosening sand from his head. At the doorstep, Skye dumped a cone-shaped pile from her shoes and then peeled off her gritty socks while Andrew banged his sneakers together. The less evidence, the better.

Inside the house, David and Veronica were waiting. "We've got to go," David said to Andrew, and the two were back out the door quickly, leaving Skye alone with her mother. Veronica curled on the couch, Leopold by her side. She looked tired. Skye greeted her with a kiss on the cheek and went to the kitchen and made tea, returning to the living room to join her mother. The house was warm and seemed eerily quiet in contrast to the screaming wind still ringing in her ears.

Skye pulled a corner of her mother's blanket onto her lap. Her body was jangly but alert, her mind clearer than it had been in two days. The experience at the beach had let loose adrenaline in her veins. Skye was emboldened, as if sharing her strange thoughts with her brother made them real. At least she wasn't alone in her head anymore. The windstorm had been alarming and affirming. What could possibly explain such ferocious wind coming out of nowhere? Maybe she wasn't crazy—maybe something crazy was happening. And if there was any chance, however farfetched, that this was connected to her mother, then something must be done.

Skye put a hand on her mother's knee. "Mom," she began, her voice soft but resolute. Her mother looked up, hearing the intention in Skye's voice. And then Skye asked out loud the single most forbidden question. "Will you tell me about Penelope?"

A startled look passed over Veronica's face and she said nothing. Skye waited, fearing that her mother would get up and leave the room or worse. She had no idea how shook up her mother had been about the clubhouse roof— maybe this was the worst possible time to ask the question.

Veronica's expression morphed, surprise fading to contemplation and then sorrow. Skye thought that her mother would start to cry. But Veronica swallowed and took a deep breath, her blue eyes cautious but calm. "Okay," she said.

Skye barreled on. "I know you don't like to talk about her, Mom. But she's on your mind."

"Yes. You're right about that."

"Tell me about her. I don't know anything. I want to know." The words came in a rush. "I want to know about her and I want to know what happened."

Skye's mother looked at the floor. "It was so hard for me when she was gone," she managed, her lip quivering. She took a deep breath and closed her eyes. "Penelope." The word hung in the air between them like a butterfly. Veronica's eyes opened. "Penelope was smart, hilarious, awkward and creative," she said. "She wrote books and songs and drew pictures and thought she was a nerd. She *was* a nerd, but the best kind. She was funny and wild and she did what she liked and didn't worry. And she was beautiful." Veronica looked at Skye. "She looked like you, Skye. She had hair just like yours."

A picture of her aunt formed in Skye's mind. "And you two were close?"

Veronica smiled and laughed, an actual laugh this time. "Yes, except for when we tried to kill each other. We were twins. *Sister* twins. It's a relationship inherently overrun with competition."

"I wouldn't know." Skye smiled.

"Having a twin sister is intimate and amazing. It's also frustrating and intense. Losing her was like…losing half of myself."

Skye watched her mother begin to retreat again. Veronica waved her hand over her heart. "Something broke."

Skye put her hand on her mother's knee. "What happened that day?"

Veronica was silent, her jaw shut tight, and her eyes flitting with memories. Finally, she spoke. "Grandpa Wolfie was the last one who saw Penelope. She came to their house—this house, before we lived here, when it was still just Wolfie and Penelope—to give him chowder after her shift at the diner. He was an old man then. She hugged him goodbye and said she was going out…The last thing he saw was her walking up Lewis Street, right outside here, along the creek."

Veronica looked towards the window, as if she could see her sister walking away. "The storm raged the next day. You were only a few days old. When I heard she was missing, I couldn't believe it. I refused to believe it. We'd lost our mother when we were so small. We barely had any time with her at all. And then Penelope. Wolfie was gone a couple of years after that…"

Veronica trailed off again. Maybe that was all that she would say. But then: "What you don't expect about grief is that it's physical. It's not a thing that can be contained, outside of you or even just in your mind. It's inside your body. Grief is an ache that takes over your whole self, and you can't find any way to ever get it out."

Veronica laid her head in Skye's lap, pulling the blanket up to her chin like she was the little girl and Skye was the mom.

Skye placed her hand on her mother's head. "I wish I would have known her."

"Me too."

Veronica dozed in Skye's lap while Skye gazed through the window into the darkening sky. From here, you could see part of the north cliffs, those rugged rust rocks that rose dramatically from the beach, topped with tall trees, and over the trees, the sky, indigo going to charcoal as dusk approached.

After a while, Veronica stirred. "I'm going to go lie down," she said. "It's been quite a day." She stood, staring at the window again, even though the view now was only dark. "By the way, the golf club roof is gone." She circled a hand lazily in the air and wandered out of the room, looking as if she might just float away.

Skye suppressed a giggle at her mother's statement—either she wasn't that shaken after all, or she was totally in shock. A few moments later, Veronica wandered back in the room, holding an envelope. "I forgot to tell you—you got a letter today." Veronica handed Skye the envelope and retreated.

Skye considered the letter in her hand. It was addressed to her at the family's address. There was no return address. The postmark read Portland, Oregon and the stamp was an illustration of a Christmas wreath.

Curious. She didn't receive much mail. Something for her birthday? But it was days away. And she didn't know anyone in Portland. She was about to open the letter when she caught sight of the clock on the wall and switched the TV on to KTSC.

Jerry Petrichor was midway through his lead story.

"...Luckily, no one was hurt today when a roof blew off at the Seafront Golf Course." A video clip launched, panning to shattered boards strewn over the greens. Skye recognized the voice of Ashley's mom, Linda, describing the storm and a gust that removed half of the clubhouse roof.

The clip ended and Jerry reappeared, speaking in a rush. "The storm retreated by 2 p.m., leaving us with a calm and quiet afternoon."

Skye's alarm bells went off. She had been listening to Jerry's voice for years, and something sounded off. Why hadn't he mentioned the wind on the beach? Or the fact that his forecast had been for calm weather, not whirlwinds strong enough to tear roofs off of buildings?

"And that's the end of another day in Starfish Cove," Jerry ended abruptly. "Have a good night, and I'll see you in the morning."

Skye switched to an old movie, but she couldn't concentrate. Why was Jerry acting weird? He hadn't even given a forecast for tomorrow—she couldn't remember him ever doing that. Telling Andrew that she felt something weird was going on, and being brave enough to talk to her mother, had been a relief. But the relief was temporary and now all she felt was anxiety again.

Skye rose from the sofa and made her way down the hall to her room, forgetting all about the letter, which slid to the floor, landing halfway under the couch.

THURSDAY, JANUARY 7, 1999
6:25 A.M.

Skye dreamt in blue. Her head swam with flashes of shimmering indigo and cerulean and sapphire, never taking any shape, remaining amorphous and out of reach. The colors were calling to her, but she didn't understand. What was she supposed to do? She tossed and turned, unsure of what was being asked of her.

Skye started awake to a hand on her shoulder. "Stormy, it's me." Andrew loomed over her, his face dimly lit by her mermaid nightlight. "Wake up. We have work to do."

She rolled over and took a peek at her digital clock. Early. She never got up this early, and Andrew definitely didn't. "What's going on?"

"Operation Fix Mom," her brother said. "We're making breakfast."

Skye sat up and reached for her hoodie and bunny slippers. Andrew spoke quietly. "I don't know what's going on with the weather—I mean, it's just *the weather*. I can't believe that it could possibly have anything to do with Mom. But yesterday, that wind at the beach...I'll admit it,

I was truly scared. If getting Mom to stop worrying has even a remote chance of preventing that from happening again, I'm in."

Skye followed her brother into the kitchen. The waffle iron was plugged in and warming, the egg skillet was on the stove with a dozen eggs sitting nearby, and a plastic carton of raspberries had been rinsed and sat on a paper towel.

"Wow," Skye said, rubbing her eyes.

"You're on eggs. I've got waffles." Andrew loaded the waffle iron with batter, hit the start button on the coffee maker, and scooted across the room to the table, which was set with nice dishes, juice glasses, and even a single silk rose in a bud vase.

"Wow," Skye repeated. Fragments of the blue entities in her dream still swam in her mind. "Sometimes you amaze me, Andrew."

"Sometimes I amaze myself, bro."

Skye had just finished the eggs when her father appeared. David Clancy took in the scene with surprise.

"I made you coffee, Dad," said Andrew.

David squinted at Andrew. "Who are you and what have you done with my son?"

Andrew grinned and poured David a cup. Skye said, "We made breakfast for Mom to cheer her up. Andrew's idea."

David lowered his eyes, taking a sip of coffee. When he lifted his face again, it was pinched with emotion. "That's so nice," he said. "I'll get her."

A few minutes later, Veronica trailed David into the

kitchen, wide-eyed, and sat at the table. She said, "There are only two place settings."

"We're going to eat in the living room," Andrew replied. "This is a romantic breakfast for two."

Skye and Andrew carried their plates to the living room and sat on the couch. Skye flipped on the television but kept the volume low, hoping to catch bits of her parent's conversation. Skye had adorned her waffle with one swipe of butter, but Andrew had doused his in tons of maple syrup, and he stuffed huge bites in his mouth.

Skye said, "Apparently being 'truly scared' hasn't impacted your appetite."

"Fueling up for battle, Stormy," he said. "No way of knowing what will happen today, and I want to be ready."

He swallowed and tiptoed over to the door, theatrically putting his ear to the wood. He nodded and smiled. "All happy noises in there. We can do magic."

"Let's hope so."

Jerry Petrichor popped onto the TV screen. "Good morning, Starfish Cove," he said. His shirt was blue, too rumpled for first thing in the morning, and he looked as if he hadn't slept.

When Skye was little, she thought Jerry lived at the TV station. He was on TV at night before she went to sleep and then again first thing in the morning—therefore, he must sleep at KTSC. Funny what crazy scenarios your mind could create when you didn't know any better.

"For those of you who haven't been outside yet, it's a perfectly peaceful morning in Starfish Cove." Jerry sounded as if he were reading from a script. Behind him on the screen, a live feed showed the pink of morning over a tranquil blue sea. The screen shifted to the map, overlaid with colors depicting precipitation, of which there was little. "The forecast looks clear, and I expect a stable day in our little Oregon Coast town." Jerry's segment came to an end, and the screen shifted to the same mattress ad Skye had seen way too many times.

She was about to reach for the curtains when their parents entered the room. "Thank you so much," said Veronica. "That was nice." Her skin was pink and she looked better than she had in days.

"You are welcome," Andrew said formally. Then, to Skye, "We must be going, dear sister. We are expected at the honorable secondary school soon."

The adults retreated to the kitchen, and Andrew danced towards his room. Skye flipped off the TV. As she stood, her foot hit something slippery. Skye looked to the floor and saw the letter that her mother had handed her last night sticking out from under her bunny slipper. She'd forgotten all about it. Skye retrieved the letter and sat back down, regarding the envelope in her hand.

She tore it open. Inside was a small piece of unlined white paper, the size of a notecard. On it, handwritten in plain script, were these words:

This weather is not an accident. It is a curse. Pay attention. Be careful. I will contact you again.

THURSDAY, JANUARY 7, 1999
8:22 A.M.

Skye stared at the notecard in her hand. Her eyes flicked over the words, reading and rereading, but still they made no sense. The weather was a curse? What did that mean? And who sent this letter? And why to her?

"Stormy!" Andrew blasted back into the living room. Skye shoved the notecard and envelope under her leg. "C'mon, bro, you're still in your pajamas. I don't want to be late."

Skye rose, concealing the papers at her side and shuffling towards the hall. She needed time to process. "Sorry, sorry, I'll be quick."

In her room, Skye pulled on jeans, a tee shirt, her hoodie and her Converse. She dashed into the bathroom and brushed her teeth. Her face in the mirror stared back at her, eyes wide in alarm.

Skye shoved the letter deep inside her backpack and headed for the front door. Andrew threw it open and Skye came to an abrupt stop.

"It's raining," she said.

"Very observant, Stormy," said Andrew, moving towards the Honda, his head ducked from the rain falling from a steel grey sky. "Can you keep moving anyway?"

"But Jerry said it was clear this morning." Skye scurried across the wet grass and ducked into the front seat of the car, pulling her hoodie over her head on the way.

"Possibly your idol Jerry was wrong," said Andrew, starting the car. "Or things changed. We live on the Oregon Coast. If you don't like the weather, wait five minutes."

Raindrops splatted across the windshield, multiplying as Andrew backed out of the drive. Skye peered into the sky, thick with grey clouds, dark and heavy with rain. A wave of panic rose inside of her as she remembered the letter in her backpack. "Seriously, Andrew!" she blurted. "What is going on?"

Her words ricocheted wild and frantic. Andrew slid her a curious look. "It's just rain, bro. It's not lightning bolts or windstorms."

"I know," she retorted. "The last couple of days have freaked me out."

Andrew made the right onto Coast Avenue, bumping up the windshield wipers a notch. Thick rivulets of water streamed down the glass. Andrew looked to the sky as if to reevaluate the downpour.

"Anyway," he said. "If anything, this proves that the weather has nothing to do with Mom. She was happy this morning. We made her *happy*." His voice rose as he attempted to convince her, or possibly just himself. "Mom is happy and it's raining anyway. So her worries don't make bad weather." He barked a laugh. "That was an insane idea, anyway."

"You said you were scared," Skye said quietly, gazing at the flooded gutters and glistening sidewalks of Coast Street, wondering if she should show Andrew the letter.

"I know," Andrew admitted. "I was. But everything is fine. It's just rain."

This weather is not an accident. It is a curse.

The words dangled in her mind, mingling with visions of blue from her dream. She closed her eyes. Was her mother cursed? Andrew would think that was crazy, and the letter, too. She needed to keep it to herself for now.

She changed the subject. "Mom and I had a conversation last night. I asked her about Penelope."

"You *what*? How did that go over?"

"Way better than I thought it might. Did you know her grandpa, Wolfie, was the last one to see Penelope alive?"

Andrew shook his head. His face was dark and brooding, and Skye had the feeling he was sick of this whole subject. She went on anyway. "Do you know how Mom's mother died?"

"No," Andrew said, pulling into a parking spot. "Mom avoids that topic even more than she does Penelope. But Dad told me once that Mom doesn't even know how her mom died—there was no one to tell her but Wolfie, and he never gave her a straight answer."

"Our family has been in Starfish Cove for decades, but we don't know anything about them," Skye said.

"We know one thing," said Andrew. "They're all dead."

His way of ending the conversation and trying to be funny at the same time, but the words slid straight into

Skye's mind like tentacles, joining with the blue from her dream and the letter in her backpack and the "curse" in a disorienting whirlwind.

Andrew exited the vehicle and slammed the door with a metallic thud, marching through puddles across the parking lot without looking back. Skye followed behind under an onslaught of raindrops slapping her in the face.

FEBRUARY 21, 1962

HEATHER BECKENDORF

Heather treasured her walks along the seashore. She loved the scent of the ocean, the breeze through her hair, and the waves sliding across the sand to break on the sand. She loved working her long legs as she walked the beautiful half-moon of Starfish Cove. In the winter, the weather could be wild and cold, with rain blowing sideways and sand whipped into the air. In the summer, it could be blessedly lovely, with clear skies and barely a breeze to cool the skin. Most of the time, it was somewhere in-between, like today—clear but cool, with a puffy bank of clouds perched offshore.

Heather loved it all. She also loved being alone. Especially now that she was mother to Penelope and Veronica, her sweet two-year-old twins, time alone was rare. She was grateful for her father, Wolfie, who loved to be with her girls. He was a gruff and fierce protector of them all in his quiet, watchful ways.

Heather walked north towards the Old Docks. Her ancestors had been fishermen, but her father never wanted anything to do with the sea. This made the broken-down docks nostalgic to Heather. She'd gaze at that motley mess of abandoned wood and spin elaborate tales of climbing aboard a boat and heading out to sea. In her mind, she'd glide over waves, cast her net deep into the sea to catch rockfish and salmon, and live free on the wild ocean.

Heather passed the Old Docks and looked ahead. Her father had forbidden her from ever climbing the treacherous trail to the top of the cliffs, but she still liked to walk to the very end of the beach and place her hands on the base of that rough rock wall. She would touch the cold, mossy stone and gaze straight up the vertical line of rock to the sky above. The view was disorienting, but thrilling—her feet planted on the sand, her imagination swirling high over the cliffs.

She gave the cliff her regards and turned back the way she'd come, towards the tide pools, her other favorite stop. She would often bring her children to explore these pools. Penelope was fair-haired and of a sunny disposition. She was the master of silly faces and small pranks, like hiding Veronica's favorite bear behind a pillow on the couch. Veronica had dark hair, and a serious manner. She had remarkable focus for a two-year-old, and could spend long periods at work on a project like stacking blocks into elaborate towers or coloring in the lines of her Mickey Mouse coloring book. Penelope seemed free and independent, while Veronica was tightly attached to both her mother and her sister, becoming sad if she was without them for even a moment.

The tide was low and the pools calm. The ocean always

moved and changed and so did the tide pools, varying by time of day, tide and season. She knew all of the creatures of the tide pool by heart. Some days she'd see the very small dark brown crabs that scurried across the bottom of the pools. Frequently, there were anemones, supple and reaching with green arms. A bit harder to find were starfish—there were one or two about if you searched, but they could be wily, clinging under an overhanging rock or tucked in a corner.

Heather made a graceful leap from the sand onto a large black rock. She hopped from rock to rock, choosing her steps carefully. She worked towards the rocky outcropping furthest from the sand and closest to the sea, where tide pools were submerged by water at higher tides. Something caught her attention, ahead in one of the larger pools. Her practiced eye identified it as a starfish, but right away something seemed off. It was large, but that wasn't so unusual. It was the color that was odd. The starfish's center was blue—a bold, deep-sea iridescent blue.

"How curious," Heather said aloud, crouching to examine the animal. It looked healthy, but had such a strange center. Heather reached a finger out to gently touch the starfish's skin. Cool and rough, as she'd have expected. There was a little surge, touching a sea creature, the feel of the cool rough exterior vibrant with life underneath. The starfish's color brightened, pulsing a bit, as if responding to her touch.

A breeze came off of the beach at Heather's back to tickle her neck. The breeze grew stronger, sending a chill up her spine and ruffling her short hair. The force of the wind increased rapidly, pushing at her back until Heather lost her balance and had to plant both hands flat on the slick rock to steady herself. The starfish continued to glow and pulse blue as she braced against the rock.

Heather let out a giggle—funny, how this strong wind had arisen from nowhere, and when she was so vulnerable, furthest from shore.

Just then, a powerful surge caught her from behind, strong enough to lift her body from the rock. Heather rose above the earth, rapidly, gracefully, lifted by the wind, her arms outstretched as if she were flying. The last thing Heather remembered was soaring away from shore above the beautiful blue sea, as free and as swift as a gull.

THURSDAY, JANUARY 7, 1999
2:30 P.M.

Skye sat in math class with a pit in her stomach and an ugly humming in her brain. As the day progressed, her eyes had been glued out the window, where a heavy rain fell. It was a dark and nasty rain, the kind that soaked into the ground until the earth resisted, sending it flooding anywhere it could go. The school lawn became a lake, trees sprouted from ponds, the street ran like a river. The rain fell in sheets so thick they lost the transparency of water and became as dark as the sky, which itself was a sullen grey.

Skye didn't agree with Andrew, that since Mom had been happy this morning, the rain proved that the weather had nothing to do with her. Sure, Veronica had seemed more cheerful this morning, but that didn't mean that the good mood had lasted. Maybe this very moment, she was back in bed with the curtains drawn. And even if she had stayed happy, that didn't mean that the damage hadn't already been done. Of course it was crazy to think that Mom's state of mind could be connected to these storms, but Andrew was too quick to dismiss the whole thing, too eager for things to be okay.

Of course, Andrew didn't know about the letter. If Mom's state of mind could be related to the storms, and a curse existed about the weather, surely, those two things were related. She slid her fingers into her hoodie pocket, feeling the smooth surface and stiff corners of the envelope and notecard. It wasn't safe leaving the letter in her backpack or in her locker—what if Ashley got ahold of it, or someone else? The letter was volatile, dangerous. *Pay attention. Be careful*, the sender had written. Until she understood more, she didn't want anyone else to know about it.

Meanwhile, the continued onslaught of water from the sky felt ominous and personal. Everything seemed more curse-like by the minute. The thing that bothered her most about the letter was that it had come to *her*. It had her name on it. Let's say there was a curse—what was she supposed to do about it?

In the afternoon, Mr. Terwilliger canceled outdoor P.E., which he hardly ever did. As a Starfish Cove old-timer, he believed in sending his students to the outdoor fields in all weather. This year already, they'd driven golf balls in driving rain and flung softballs that came up from the ground slippery with mud.

But today, he kept them in. Not only that, he didn't even make them do a zillion pull-ups or endless laps around the gym. Instead, he put on music, asked the students to do simple floor stretches, and disappeared. Normally, Skye would have been happy for the mellow day, but today it added to her angst. Even Mr. Terwilliger seemed to have lost his mind.

Ashley seemed unimpressed by both the weather and the turn of events in P.E. She sat splay-legged on the gym floor next to Skye, wearing fuchsia leopard print leggings. She'd paired them with a turquoise blue ruffled top and her denim jacket, which still had pink smoothie on the sleeve from yesterday. Now she stared out the gym window with a disgusted look on her face.

"Gross," Ashley said. "Why didn't Mom decide to move to Arizona instead of this dumb town? I can't believe I have to grow up in a place where you can't even go outside without *drowning*."

Skye rolled her eyes, stretching her fingers towards her toes. "I think that's a bit of an exaggeration."

Ashley twisted her mouth. "Like I could ever convince you. You're totally brainwashed into thinking the weather here is awesome. You'd be bored out of your mind in Arizona—not enough drama."

Under normal conditions, Skye would have agreed with this point. Today, that clutch of dread in her middle led her to believe that a little less drama might be okay.

Ashley went on. "The weather in Starfish Cove *kills* people. That doesn't happen in Arizona."

"What are you talking about?" Skye sighed.

Ashley pointed out the window. "Some old guy got struck dead by lightning right on top of the north cliffs."

An unsettling zing shot through Skye's middle. "When?"

"It was a long time ago. He lived up in an old cabin

85

where the hotel used to be."

Skye tingled with alarm. She knew about that cabin. "How did you hear about this?"

"Mom. And Jerry. They are completely obsessed with these storms, and how they came out of nowhere. Did you know this weather is only right here? Not anywhere else in the whole state? Jerry's freaking out because he can't figure out what's going on and Mom is all paranoid-conspiracy-theory. She started digging into things that happened a long time ago, like some lady who went missing from the beach 30 years ago. And the guy who was struck by lightning." Ashley added, "See? What's so great about Starfish Cove? You might die here."

Mr. Terwilliger reappeared as a memory unfurled in Skye's mind. It was a sunny spring day last year when Mr. Terwilliger took P.E. to the beach. "Let's get outside," he said. "Let's run wild on the beach like true Oregon Coast residents."

The 7th graders had mostly been happy to be set loose on the shore, except Ashley, who complained immediately about sand in her shoes. Mr. Terwilliger had them run to the Old Docks, where they paused, waiting for stragglers. Skye could see Ashley dragging herself up the beach, staring at her feet with irritation.

One of the boys said, "Let's go up there," pointing to a steep and rocky cut up the north cliff.

"Bad idea, Jones," Mr. Terwilliger replied. "That trail hasn't been safe for years. But do you know what used to be up there?"

Jones didn't seem to know. Skye did, but studied the

gulls over the water rather than respond. "Hotel Starfish Cove," Mr. Terwilliger explained. He told the students about the luxurious hotel, built in 1893 to service the well-off tourists who came from Portland on the passenger railroad. The hotel was an impressive structure of brick and wood, with a sweeping veranda overlooking the sea. "It changed Starfish Cove's economy and significance for over 50 years, but our city's reputation as a summer destination changed forever when Hotel Starfish Cove burned to the ground in 1932."

"All that remained was the caretaker's cabin." Mr. Terwilliger scanned the students before him until his eyes settled on Skye. "And one of our classmates knows all about that. Ms. Clancy?" Skye froze, pasting a blank look on her face and waiting for Mr. Terwilliger to make sense. "Her great uncle Bertram Beckendorf was the caretaker of Hotel Starfish Cove. He stayed on for another decade to mind the property after the hotel fire."

Skye smiled blandly. She didn't know anything about that. She hadn't even heard her great-uncle's name before. To deflect the eyes pinned on her, she turned her attention to Ashley, who meandered down the beach at a snail's pace.

It wasn't any surprise Skye had never learned that her family had a connection to the hotel, given her mother's reticence to talk about any of it. Still, Mr. Terwilliger's tidbit of information explained one thing—why her mother had always forbade her from going near the cliffs. From the time she was itty bitty, Veronica had made Skye and Andrew promise they would stay away from the dangerous north cliffs. And Skye kept her promise. How many times had she walked that beach? Hundreds. And she'd never climbed that cliff.

Skye's attention came back to Ashley sprawled before her on the gym floor. According to Ashley, Skye's great-uncle had been killed by lightning. Was he part of this curse?

The final bell rang and Skye left the gym with her shoulders hunched and her hand clutched around the letter in her pocket. Ashley shot her a questioning look, but Skye didn't feel like explaining anything to anybody. Never in her life had she dreaded going outside, let alone wished to be anywhere other than Starfish Cove. But nothing was right or safe today.

Pay attention. Be careful. I will contact you again. All she could do was wait.

THURSDAY, JANUARY 7, 1999
3:30 P.M.

Skye walked out of school straight into a disaster area. The parking lot had flooded and was now an ankle deep swimming pool of cold Oregon Coast rain. The storm raged. Raindrops pelted her cheeks and a fierce wind grabbed at her hair. Skye yanked her rain jacket out of her backpack and shoved her arms inside, squeezing the coat around her middle and bracing herself against the scene.

Andrew appeared at her side. "Another undeniably delightful day in Oregon's coastal gem of a city, Starfish Cove," he intoned. He took a flying leap off of the staircase, landing with a giant splash in a puddle. Andrew held his arms overhead, Broadway-style.

Skye was still jittery and worried and wished he would be too. But she knew he was trying to make her laugh, and she was glad for the distraction. "Where's your coat?" she asked.

"I forgot it," he hollered enthusiastically into the sky.

"You had it this morning."

"True story, Stormy. Is it in the band room or the math

room? In the art studio or in my locker? Only time will tell, and the truth is, we may never know the truth." Andrew's shoes were completely covered by water, and his Henley shirt was soaked to the skin already.

"You are such a dork."

"Also true, Stormy." Andrew shook his whole body head to toe and waved his arms in the air again. "Okay, I'm wet. Let's say goodbye to Starfish Cove Secondary, at least for today."

He bolted towards the Honda and Skye followed. Students scurried out of the building and into the weather, some silently, some complaining. Lucy, her brother's recent love interest, tiptoed through the deluge in capris and ballerina flats, squealing like a lion was chasing her. A junior boy in a football jersey followed her closely, mumbling placating words and trying to put his arm around her, but Lucy flailed too wildly to let his arm land anywhere. Skye suppressed a giggle, and Andrew shot her an eye roll over his shoulder.

Andrew slid into home at the driver's door, unlocking the car, leaping in and reaching across to flip the lock on Skye's side. She jerked open the door and climbed in. Andrew fired up the engine and declared, "And we're off!"

Nothing happened.

Finally, the Honda made a meager cough and lurched across the flooded pavement, the engine gaining momentum as they put-putted out of the parking lot. Andrew flipped on the tape deck and the sounds of The Cure filled the car. He navigated the Honda through downtown, heading for home. The streets ran thick with water. The sky was the color of a dirty nickel, and the windshield wipers worked hard to keep up with the rain.

Andrew made the turn onto Main Street. From a distance, Skye spotted the bridge that crossed Lewis Creek. It was tough to see through the curtain of rain, but as they approached, something looked weird. Andrew slowed the car. The bridge rails looked normal, solid steel and wood, but the concrete surface wavered before her eyes. As they approached, she couldn't quite bring the bridge into focus—it rippled and glistened. Skye squinted, trying to make sense of what she saw.

"So that's what it looks like when the creek floods," Andrew said.

Skye understood—the bridge surface looked strange because it wasn't concrete, it was water. Water over concrete. What they saw was a steady flow of creek water sliding under the bridge rails over the bridge surface.

"Whoa," Skye said.

Now that she knew what she was looking at, it was strangely clear. Silvery water pushed towards the sea over whatever was in its path. It was oddly beautiful, and Skye was transfixed.

"I'm going to check it out," Andrew said, reaching for the car door.

"No! Don't go out there!" Skye reached for her brother.

Andrew pulled away as the door flung open into the storm. "I'm already wet, what's the worst that can happen?" He leapt outside, hollering, "I'm just going to take a peek!"

The door slammed shut, dampening the sound of the

storm and leaving Skye alone in the quiet. Andrew sprinted towards the bridge, throwing up splashes of water with his footsteps. The pit of dread in her stomach expanded into an ocean of panic as the space between them grew. Her body tightened in a nervous clench.

Skye leaned forward, peering through the wet windshield and wild stormy air. Andrew had grabbed ahold of the west rail and inched his way onto the bridge. A foot of water covered his feet.

What an idiot! She should have told him about the letter, she should have told him about the curse. Skye was sweating and cold at the same time. Should she go outside, and haul him back to the car? Should she yell at him through the howling wind, and beg him to come back?

Before she could make a decision, Andrew disappeared. In less than a second, her brother was there, leaning over the rail, and then he was gone.

Skye moaned and blinked, daring it to not be true. It must be a trick of her eyes, an effect of the murky, rainy sky. One more blink and he would be there. No. She scanned the area, frantic, but there was no Andrew. On the bridge was nothing but a steady flow of water.

Skye sat for one more frozen second and then exploded out of the Honda, running at a full sprint towards the creek.

THURSDAY, JANUARY 7, 1999
4:01 P.M.

Skye reached the bridge in seconds. Rain and wind pummeled her as she sloshed through water. She made it to the place where Andrew had stood and gripped the sodden rail, peering into the swollen waters. What she saw confirmed her worst fears.

The water was turbulent and murky and moving fast. Andrew's yellow tee-shirt stood out against the gloom. Her brother floated downstream a couple of hundred yards, moving with the current towards the sea. A creek that was normally only deep enough to wade in now raged a river, carrying her brother swiftly with it.

"Andrew!" Skye screamed in a hollow wail. "Andrew!"

Skye flew to the end of the bridge and ran alongside the creek. She knew the creek bank well—thick with alder and salal, it was followed by a narrow trail packed down by the feet of local children who went looking for water skippers and pollywogs.

But all of this was underwater now.

Through the tops of the drowned shrubs, she saw her

brother's head floating downstream, the tips of his shoes poking out of the water. At least he was still above water; at least he could still breathe.

"Andrew!" She gained on him, fearing the roar of the water and wind carried her voice away. Skye's raincoat flew open around her, rain soaking her hoodie. Her Converse were soggy and her drenched hair slapped at her neck. But she didn't care.

What was downstream? Eventually this stream reached the beach, cutting a small valley through the dune and then washing over sand in a shallow fan that dissolved into the ocean. At least that's what normally happened. Who knew what this flood would do as it reached the sea?

Skye slammed down the wet street, winding around parked cars, until she caught up to where her brother drifted in the current.

"Andrew!" She galloped to keep up with his trajectory. His head was still above water but his skin was white and chalky. She screamed his name one more time at the top of her lungs and he turned his head her way. He reached a hand out of the water, opening his mouth to call out something that she couldn't make out.

Skye scanned the ground for something to help Andrew. He was floating past the tops of alders, but none of the branches were sturdy enough for him to grab ahold of. A long stick appeared up ahead and she considered tossing it to him, but what if she missed? What if he couldn't reach it or she hit him with it?

She didn't trust herself to pull him back to shore—she wasn't sure the stick was long enough or she was strong enough. Everything was happening so fast—she didn't have time to think anything through.

Skye knew where she was—only another block until the dune. Anxiety rose in her throat. What if Andrew swept into one of the large shore pine that grew on this side of the dune? What if he slammed into the rocky creek bed as the water gushed towards the sand? She tried to remember the tide schedule for today. What if it was high tide, and the flooding waters washed her brother directly out to sea?

Skye side-stepped down the street, keeping an eye on her brother, her lungs burning and sweat mixing with rainwater on her brow.

Ahead appeared the horizon line, the bright streak that hung between dark churning sea and black rainy sky. The street ended and Skye's feet hit dirt as the creek continued to rage past her, the high water pushing hard towards the ocean, pulling Andrew ahead of her once more and beyond the dune out of Skye's sight.

She tore her way up a hill of soft wet sand, clawing through beach grass to drop off onto the other side. Skye came to a stop at the sight of the turmoil below.

The creek powered around the corner and crashed into a raging high tide that pushed sea onto shore. The force of the collision threw huge surges of water skyward to mingle with heavy rain falling from overhead. Wind whipped up the shore and pushed Skye backwards as rain pelted her eyes. Where was Andrew?

Her eyes scanned the frothing water, searching for a swath of yellow. The violent waters revealed nothing, and terror swam through her blood. A flock of seagulls banked over the surf, fighting the wind to stay on the wing. She perched on top of the dune and held back panic as tears swelled in her throat.

"Andrew," she whispered, thinking terrible thoughts of him under the heavy surf, struggling for his life. Skye was soaked and cold and afraid. She put her head in her hands and sobbed. How had all of this happened? The curse must be real. It was horribly, awfully real.

She raised her head from her hands as tears poured down her face, mixing with rainwater and salty air. She could barely see anything now, through the storm and her tears. She looked down the churning beach towards the Old Docks and cursed this—the beach, her home—the very place she loved and had always given her solace.

Suddenly, a flash of yellow. Skye swiped at her eyes. Yes, there, at the crux of the creek and the tideline, tucked behind a large piece of driftwood—yellow. Andrew's yellow tee-shirt.

Skye slid down the sand and ran to her brother. He had collapsed on his belly, arms splayed. Skye fell to his side. His clothes were drenched and plastered to his clammy skin. His cheek was to the sand and his eyes were closed.

"Andrew," Skye pulled his hair away from his eyes. His back rose as he took a breath. "Andrew," she said again, desperately.

One of his eyes popped open. Andrew rolled over and sat up, sand and woody debris clinging to his shirt and arms.

"Stormy," he blurted, spitting sand from his mouth and swiping at his ruined clothing. "Why did you make me go out on that bridge? You're always trying to get me to do dumb things."

Skye threw her arms around her brother's sandy, salty neck and gave him a kiss on the cheek as the wind whipped the frothy water upon them.

JANUARY 15, 1985

PENELOPE BECKENDORF

The storms had been raging for over a week. Penelope made her way up the woodsy trail that led to the top of the north cliffs. For eight days now, torrential rain, hail, lightning, wind and high surf had pummeled Starfish Cove. At first, it had been easy to shrug the storms off as a bad spell at the Oregon Coast. It was January, after all, and winter storms were to be expected. Penelope and her co-workers at the Chowder Bowl had come to work each evening soaked, laughing, and sharing stories of the challenges of navigating their shabby cars through flooded streets and how their cats had been staying inside for days on end, which cats just don't do. *Isn't it crazy,* they said. *When will it ever stop,* they asked.

But after a week, the storms were less amusing and more daunting. To Penelope, the weather was beginning to verge on frightening. In her 26 years in Starfish Cove, Penelope had never experienced anything like she had in the previous days. Consider the wind that blew down the Chowder Bowl sign the night she was there alone closing up, for instance. She'd been seconds from locking up the front door and heading home into the night when the sign came crashing down with an enormous slam to the sodden earth. It left a divot the size of a grave. Half a minute later and she would have been standing in that very spot. It had scared Penelope half to death, and she wasn't one to scare easily.

And next came the hailstorm, a few days later. She'd been walking home from a friend's house, a little bit too late, but that wasn't unusual. She knew her way home to Grandpa Wolfie's like the back of her hand. Sure, it was stormy, but was there truly any danger?

The answer to that question came by way of hailstones the size of her head—or her fist, anyway. She'd been walking along Main Street when out of nowhere gigantic hailstones fell from the sky. Penelope gasped. Weather conditions of all sorts she'd seen, but she'd never been hit by something from the sky large enough to hurt.

Penelope had begun to run, her feet skittering clumsily over the slippery layer of hail on wet pavement. The hail kept up as she made her way home under a steady pounding of pellets. She was beginning to feel spooked, as if the weather was a ghost following her around with the intent to do her harm.

Penelope reached the little house she shared with her grandfather with hailstones still clinging to her clothing. It was only Penelope and Wolfie here, now, since Veronica had married and moved out a few years before. Just a few days ago, Veronica had given birth to her second child—a little girl. Penelope visited the hospital, wading through a flooded parking lot to get inside, and held that tiny baby, named Skye for the storms she was born under.

Penelope had blasted out of the hail and in the front door, finding Wolfie still awake, as he frequently was late at night. He had given her an odd look, as if her haunted feeling was reflected in his eyes.

Now, she emerged from the woods onto the cliff top and the overgrown trail that followed the rim. When they were little, Wolfie had been emphatic that she and Veronica never go to the north cliffs. As a child, Penelope obeyed. But as she grew older and her daily explorations of their small town expanded, she became curious. She loved the wild forest, the wind-whipped trees, the birds soaring on currents of air, the thick salal, the views west over the grand sea. Why not find a way to climb to the top of the world, where the forest would surely be lush and the views expansive and no one but her around to enjoy it?

The steep rocky trail that led from the beach to the old hotel site had long ago eroded away. But years ago, Penelope set out to find a way to reach the cliffs. Turns out if she followed the creek upstream, above the bridge, and wound through the forest on deer paths, and paid attention to the location of the sea and the sky, and climbed steadily through pine and salal, she could reach the cliff and its wild trails. Penelope went alone. Year after year, the trails and the cliff became her secret getaway.

And where she was now, despite the weather. Almost *to* spite the weather—Penelope needed to prove to herself that she could still climb to her favorite trail, that she wasn't afraid. It was raining, but she had a jacket. No one on the

Oregon Coast used umbrellas—they were impractical in the wind. A slicker with a hood pulled tight—that would do. Penelope pushed up the hill beyond the creek and emerged at the top of the cliff to a forceful wind. She smiled. This was the familiar energy she loved—wind, rain and ocean, each creating power that invigorated her, even if it meant she was cold and wet and tired at journey's end.

Penelope tore down the trail to the clearing where the old hotel had been, and where great-uncle Bertram's ramshackle cabin still sat. In all of her years of exploring, she never approached the old boarded-up cabin, out of respect for Wolfie's cautions or her own creepy feeling about the place, she wasn't sure. She snuck a look as she passed—the broken down structure was dark through the murky windows.

A few yards past the cabin came a sound like a whip cracking. Penelope's sneakers skidded in mud to a sudden halt. Just as quickly, the sky fell. Or that's how it seemed.

An enormous shore pine slammed to the ground right at Penelope's feet. It was as if the earth had risen to meet it, the two bodies of mass meeting in a crashing explosion of wood and soil. Splinters of wood broke free from the trunk and flew at her body like tiny darts. Mud and dirt lifted from the ground and splattered her clothing and face. The tree hit the edge of the cliff and broke in two, its top half tumbling down the cliff and crashing into the sea below. Penelope froze, every cell in her body ignited, and completely lost her breath.

THURSDAY, JANUARY 7, 1999

4:35 P.M.

Skye lay with her cheek against her brother's chest, feeling the rise and fall of his lungs until she believed he was alive. Andrew was soaked, dirty and coated in sand. He coughed and took in raspy breaths of air. Skye kept her eyes closed as the whistle of his breath mingled with the erratic crash of the high surf and the gurgle of the stream at high flow.

Surely, the curse was real. Images of Andrew caught in the current ricocheted in her mind, the feeling of panic returning full force. Of course a stream could run high during a big rain event, but for it to crest a bridge and capture her brother was just too much.

Skye threw her eyes open and sat up to shake off the fear. Andrew sat up too, flinging sand from his fingertips and swiping at his face with the back of his hand.

The scene where the creek met the tide was epic. A dirty-white foam had been whipped up by the weather and now flew in thick sticky clumps into the air. A glob of dense sea foam rose up in a gust of wind and hit Skye right in the eye.

She laughed. The sea foam was weird, but less threatening than a flooding creek or whirlwind. She turned her head to shake the foam from her face and saw two figures approaching. They were coming quickly, and one of them carried a large object. She blinked until the foam slid away from her eyes.

"Skye, is that you?" called Ashley's mom as she scurried down the dune. Her red hair tousled in the wind and her glasses were smeared with rain. "Are you okay?" With her was Jerry Petrichor, who toted a television camera awkwardly on one shoulder, filming as he stumbled over the uneven sand. He was wearing the same shirt as this morning, only now it was rumpled and wet.

Linda reached the Clancys and dipped to one knee on the beach. "We heard someone fell in the creek. What happened?"

Skye was dizzy. She hadn't even processed that Andrew had nearly drowned—now her idol Jerry was four feet away, not only witnessing her state of disaster, but filming it too. This wasn't exactly how she envisioned participating in a weather report. "It was Andrew," she managed. "My brother Andrew fell in the creek."

"Are either of you hurt?" asked Linda.

"Just my pride," said Andrew, who had begun to shiver.

"Let's get you home," said Jerry, extending his hand to Skye and helping her to her feet. A shiver ran through her, too, but she wasn't sure it was because she was cold.

A few minutes later, Linda and Jerry helped Skye and

Andrew through the foam, wind and rain to the KTSC truck, which sat in the small lot over the beach dune.

Skye had seen this truck many times, with its large blue and green logo painted across the side and the tall antenna on top. The vehicle was old and beat-up, and nothing like a TV truck you'd find in the city, but it was still amazing to Skye. She'd dreamed one day she'd step inside, but hadn't imagined her first ride would be a rescue taxi trip while she was dripping wet and covered in sea foam.

The inside of the van was as she had imagined, but way better, with black leather seats and high-tech equipment tucked securely into shelving. Jerry and Linda didn't hesitate before loading two soggy, sand-covered kids inside. Jerry fired up the engine and the heater and turned to Andrew and Skye. Skye tried not to stare, that handsome face in person, the way his eyes pinched at the sides in concern.

"Do you need anything? Are you hungry?" Jerry asked, adding, "Do you want pistachio nuts?"

Linda rolled her eyes. "Inside joke. He's trying to be funny."

"I'm usually the smart aleck," said Andrew, who shook hard now from the damp and chill.

The Clancy home was only ten blocks from the beach and the creek. Skye just wanted to get home and tell Andrew about the letter so he could help her figure out what to do. Jerry came around the corner of Lewis and Clark at a fast clip, swinging the van to a rollicking stop on the gravel driveway.

Skye held her breath, studying her house and waiting

for her parents to come spilling out. But the curtains were drawn, and the door stayed shut.

Linda turned from the front seat. "Do you want us to talk to your parents?" she asked.

"No," both Skye and Andrew replied in unison. "It's okay," Skye added, trying to sound nonchalant. "We can tell them what happened."

The two piled out, waving goodbye to Jerry and Linda as the KTSC rig jostled down the street towards the station. Andrew and Skye paused in front of the house, exchanging a thousand thoughts without saying anything.

Finally, Skye released a short laugh. "You look like someone who almost drowned in a creek today."

"Weird." Andrew's curly hair stuck up in all directions, his shirt hung sodden, and a layer of sand coated his head. "You don't look so hot yourself."

Skye's hair had come loose again and was shot through with bits of sea foam.

Andrew murmured, "This is going to scare the hell out of Mom."

Skye nodded, thinking their mother was going to be a whole lot more frightened when she found out she was under a curse. "Maybe she won't find out," she said.

Andrew smiled at Skye. "Stormy," he said. "We're going to be on TV."

Skye had already forgotten about the TV camera. Her mind was muddled, as if she experienced the world with one eye shut and one hand over an ear and a gang of butterflies in her chest.

Andrew took a deep breath and pushed the front door

open gingerly, bracing for the full parental freak-out. But the living room was dark and quiet. The siblings waited as time ticked by. A door creaked at the end of the hall and David approached his children, speaking quietly. "Hey, glad you're home. Your mom's having a rough night. She had a panic attack this afternoon. I put her to bed a while ago. I need to get back to her—make yourselves some dinner."

David hustled back down the hall.

"But she seemed better this morning." Andrew looked at the floor. "I thought she was better." He sounded like a little boy, hope lilting in his voice.

Skye put one hand on her brother's arm and reached the other into her pocket. It was time to tell him what was going on.

But before she could pull the letter out, Andrew said, "Stormy! We forgot the Honda!" He turned for the door.

"Wait! You'll never make it over the bridge."

"I'll go the long way, up around Pine Street. It'll be fine." And he was gone.

"Be careful," Skye said to an empty room. She listened to the rain on the old house's roof. Rain had always been such a soothing sound, but now it only made her wonder what was coming next.

She sighed and turned for the shower. As she passed the table by the hall, a flash of white caught her eye. There lay a plain white envelope.

She stared at the letter without touching it. On the front, her name and address, no return address, Christmas stamp, and Portland post mark.

A shiver passed through her and she snatched the letter, moving swiftly towards her bedroom. She shut the door and sat on the bed, tearing the envelope open with trembling fingers.

Inside was a rectangle of plain white paper, the size of a notecard. The handwriting was the same.

The glow of the starfish is the origin of the curse. She who saw the glow is the center of the storms. Seek answers at Bertram's cabin.

THURSDAY, JANUARY 7, 1999
7:09 P.M.

Skye sat on her bed and clutched the note. Her familiar bedroom—the checkered quilt, the mermaid lamp, the photos of sandy beaches—all swam garish and frightening before her eyes. Her heart pounded and her body shook.

The glow of the starfish is the origin of the curse. She who saw the glow is the center of the storms.

"She" wasn't Veronica. "She" was Skye. Skye had seen the starfish. Her mother wasn't the center of the storms. Skye was. Her mind spun wildly now, the starfish with the blue center swirling in dizzying circles in her memory.

It seemed like a dream. It was days ago. She'd forgotten all about it. Monday. The day before the storms began. Now the moment came back to her in a vivid, sickening flash. Her science class had taken a field trip to the aquarium. The old aquarium, which had occupied a storefront on Main Street since the time of Hotel Starfish Cove. The destination was small and not very exciting. But it was what Starfish Cove had, and each year their teachers found a reason to visit.

Skye had been wandering the exhibits with her

classmates, tasked out to survey the animals and identify which part of the marine ecosystem they would naturally inhabit. Beach, tidal zone, intertidal zone, deep-water zone. Skye and Ashley had passed the touch table, a shallow pool of seawater and rocks like a tide pool, when something caught Skye's eye.

The starfish was large, and deeply textured, with a rugged and mottled look to its orange exterior. But what was striking was the center of the animal, which glowed a subtle iridescent blue.

Skye took a second look. Was it an effect of the aquarium lighting? A trick of the eye? No. The blue light came and went, pulsing but unmistakable.

Ashley had noticed Skye pause, and looked at her quizzically.

"Do you see that?" Skye asked.

"Yes, Clancy, it's a starfish," Ashley had replied. "I believe you've seen them before."

Skye observed the starfish. She was sure she saw a blue glow. But did she? A glowing starfish was crazy. Obviously Ashley didn't see anything unusual. So maybe Skye didn't either.

"Let's go." Ashley was tugging at her sleeve. *It must have been an optical illusion,* Skye concluded, and then forgot all about it.

Now, the starfish burned bright in her mind. She didn't doubt the blue glow anymore. She had seen it and it was real. She thought of the dreams she'd had all week—blue visions, beseeching her in her sleep.

The weather was a curse, the first note declared. *The*

glow of the starfish is the origin of the curse, read the second note. And finally, *She who saw the glow is the center of the storms.*

All of this time, Skye had been worrying about her mother. But it wasn't her mother who made the storms. It was her. Skye had seen the starfish. If the person who saw the starfish was cursed, and the curse made the terrifying weather, then Skye was responsible for the storms.

The last few days rushed through her mind. The traffic light that swung at the truck. The whirlwind that hit the golf course. The wind that blew her and Andrew off of the beach. The flooded creek that Andrew nearly drowned in.

No one else in town had experienced these dangers. It was her family who had been threatened, and in every situation, Skye was present. If she was the one who was cursed, she was to blame. Because of Skye, her parents had barely escaped a falling roof. Because of Skye, her brother had been swept away by a surging creek.

And someone else also thought Skye was cursed—the mysterious letter writer. Why else would the letters be addressed to her? Skye's mind whirled, trying to make sense of the situation. How could this be happening? Four days ago, she was a normal girl, and now she was cursed by a glowing starfish that made the sky go crazy and tried to kill her family.

She thought of Andrew, sliding out of her reach into the treacherous waters of the creek. She had to stop this. *Seek answers at Bertram's cabin.* She didn't even know where Bertram's cabin was, not really. But she had to go there. She had to know what the notes meant. Skye sat on her

110

bed, clutching her pillow and shaking.

The front door of the house clicked open and shut. Andrew, returning from retrieving the Honda. Abruptly, she stood from her bed and crossed to the door. She needed to tell her brother what was going on. She needed help.

But she couldn't tell Andrew. She couldn't put him in more danger. She couldn't tell anyone. As long as she was cursed, anyone near her was at risk. Skye had to solve this problem by herself.

She sank to a heap on her bedroom floor. *I'm so scared. I'm so alone.* Outside, a gust of wind slammed at the house, the pressure pushing against her bedroom window. A high-pitched whistle screamed over the rooftop and suddenly she was filled with energy and purpose. The energy of the storm was within her now, pushing her to act.

Skye rose and went to the closet. She changed out of her wet clothes into a dry outfit, and then found her backpack. She shoved a sweatshirt inside, and her spare raincoat. From her bedside table, she grabbed the flashlight that she used when she wanted to read under the covers late at night. She tucked that in the backpack too. She located both mysterious letters and folded them into the pack's outside pocket. Then she shut off the light and crawled under the covers with all of her clothes on except her shoes, and waited.

Andrew tapped on her door at some point. She pretended to be asleep. She heard her father in the bathroom, and the latch of the door when he returned to her mother. After a while, Andrew's music shut off, and his lamp switch clicked. She waited a little longer. Her body was rigid and her mind on fire.

Once Skye was sure everyone was asleep, she rose. She tied her Converse on and lifted her backpack quietly from the floor. She crept to the kitchen, where she filled a water bottle and slid open a kitchen drawer and removed two granola bars. Those, too, she tucked in her backpack.

Leopold brushed up against her legs, mewling quietly. Skye bent to pet his soft fur and wondered when she would see him again. Then she slipped out the sliding glass door into the dark and stormy night.

JANUARY 15, 1985

PENELOPE BECKENDORF

After the tree fell, and once Penelope recovered from the fright of coming close to being crushed by a falling pine, she stood for the longest time, observing the obstacle in her path.

Trees looked weird when they were suddenly sideways on the ground. They weren't supposed to be that way. The bark that had been 15 feet in the air was now two feet from her nose. The thing was, it was extraordinarily beautiful. Delicate lichen clung to the knobby bark. The grooves in the surface of the tree were deep and intricate, like a little artful world that had only moments ago been high overhead.

Penelope admired the beauty, but slowly, fear crept back in. She could have been crushed. She could have died right here. No one would have even known where she was—it might have taken days for anyone to find her. Why did the tree fall here, right as she passed? That creepy feeling returned, that somehow the bad weather was all about her.

A quick breeze came up and slivers of fear slid under

Penelope's skin. She turned abruptly on her heel and ran down the trail through the woods. She ran for home. She couldn't carry these suspicions alone anymore. She remembered that strange look in Wolfie's eyes the other day, after the hailstorm. Penelope needed to talk to her grandfather.

Penelope burst through the door of the small house she shared with Wolfie. She hadn't bothered to remove her coat or boots, and now rainwater dripped on the kitchen floor. Her grandfather sat at the small blue table. He looked up sharply from the sketch in pencil he had been working on all day.

"Girl, what has come over you? You're making a mess of the floor." Wolfie's grey hair sprouted from his head every which way, but his blue eyes were kind even as he scolded her. Wolfie peered into her eyes and his tone changed from annoyed to concerned. "Penny, you look like you've seen a ghost. Are you alright?"

"Not really, grandpa," she said. "A tree fell."

He looked at her, not understanding. "Tell me more."

Penelope sank into a chair. In stilted words, she explained her strange feelings—how the weather was following her around, how she felt quite haunted. She spilled a jumble of words onto the table between them: the sign at the Oyster, the hailstorm, and the tree.

Wolfie's aged face was creased with concern. When she was done, he rose and put on the kettle.

"I'm going to make us tea," he said. "I want you to change your clothes, and let your mind rest a bit, and think if anything out of the ordinary happened before all of this began."

Penelope rose, but before she crossed the threshold, she turned abruptly. "The starfish."

Wolfie nodded, as if he had already known what she was going to say. "Are you frozen to the bone, girl?"

"No. I feel like I'm on fire."

Wolfie turned the kettle off. "Then we're going back up that hill. I need to show you something. I always feared it would come to this, but hoped with all my heart that it wouldn't." He reached for his worn slicker by the door. "You can tell me what happened when we get there."

Five minutes later, Penelope followed her grandfather up a trail she didn't even know he knew about. This was her secret trail on the other side of the creek, but he navigated the thick forest as if he did it every day. Wolfie pushed branches aside, holding them out of her way as they climbed up the muddy hill towards the cliff.

She skittered behind him as she always did when she was a little girl, trying to keep up with his confident stride. "What's going on, Grandpa?" she asked, but he kept climbing, his strength contradicting his 87 years of age.

Penelope had forgotten all about seeing that strange starfish. She wondered how on earth such an odd occurrence could have slipped her mind. But something fuzzy had muddled her memory, and then the crazy weather hit, and was enough distraction to shake the starfish loose from her brain.

They reached the top of the trail, and the ocean came into view. The wind blew hard, and Penelope's long blond hair flew behind her head like a silvery flag. She pointed along the length of the cliff. "The tree is down there."

"You can show me later." Wolfie pointed at great-uncle Bertram's cabin. "We're going there."

Penelope didn't understand. Wolfie had always told her to avoid the cliffs and especially the cabin, where his cantankerous uncle had lived most of his life. She'd broken the rules about the cliffs, but never approached the cabin, which even now looked spooky, dangerous, and liable to collapse on her head. But she followed her grandfather as he fought through a thicket of salal and blackberry towards the strange old cabin.

The windows were streaked with years of raindrops and dirt. The inside of the cabin was dark through the murky windows. The front steps were half-caved in, and the front door had two large boards nailed over it, like a giant do-not-enter sign. Wolfie reached the building and kept going, disappearing around the back only to reappear immediately with a crowbar. He pried each board from its position. He pulled the door open as if it was his very own, stepped over the broken first step, and disappeared inside.

Penelope hesitated. "C'mon, girl," Wolfie called from the dark interior. She took a deep breath, and stepped through the doorway.

Inside was gloomy and smelled of mildew. In the shadows were the shapes of abandoned furniture. On the back wall of the main room rested a large stone fireplace. From the inside, the windows were lit up as bright squares of daylight, splashing rectangles of opaque light on the dusty floorboards.

"Why are we here?" Penelope shivered in her damp

clothes.

"Tell me about the starfish, Penny."

She'd been down by the Old Docks, two weeks ago, on a calm day—the last nice day that Starfish Cove had seen since. She'd been puttering around on the rocks by the tide pools, thinking about nothing in particular and all sorts of things at the same time. Something caught her eye, something like a flash of blue. She hopped a couple of rocks, moving in the direction of what she'd seen. In a tide pool were a few urchins, anemones and one large starfish. Penelope crouched down and startled when the starfish lit up, radiating an iridescent blue light from its center. After a moment, the light subsided, only to return a minute later.

"It was very weird," she recounted now to her grandfather, whose eyes were pinned on her. "There was no one else around. I felt a little light-headed. I made my way to work and forgot all about it."

A stiff gust of wind rattled the old wooden walls. Penelope wrapped her arms around her middle as her grandfather regarded her in the weak light. Wolfie reached into his pocket and pulled out a flashlight, the sudden beam of light glancing off of the walls erratically as he turned towards the back of the house. "Follow me."

Being careful not to trip on anything, Penelope followed Wolfie through the kitchen to a blue door with a brass knob. They entered what she imagined had been Bertram's bedroom. Wolfie beckoned with the flashlight, and Penelope came up to his side. He fixed the light on the back wall, illuminating a painted shape.

Penelope squinted in the dark but couldn't quite

make out the image. Wolfie pulled his arm back until the flashlight beam encompassed the entire painting, then he flipped the light to its high beam and the colors and shapes of the image came clearly into view.

Penelope gasped. Before her, covering the entire wall, was a painting of a starfish. A crude drawing, but the shape was plain as day. The creature's body was a mottled orange, as if someone had taken a paintbrush and smashed it into the wall over and over again. At the starfish's center, the color was blue. No ordinary blue—here the artist had taken great care, creating a precise turquoise blue and dappling it with points of silvery white. With the wavering flashlight, the blue center of the starfish seemed to pulse just as it had in real life.

"Your great uncle Bertram became obsessed with starfish before he died," Wolfie explained. "Not all starfish, but this one particular starfish with an illuminated, blue center that he claimed he'd seen. He tried to talk to me about it. Bertram felt that the starfish had done him wrong. He'd had a string of bad luck related to the weather and believed it was related."

"I thought he was out of his mind. He was always so eccentric, ranting about all sorts of things. One day, it was too many fishermen; the next day, not enough fish; the next day, the weather. I had become accustomed to ignoring him, and when he told me he was cursed, I dismissed him entirely." The lines in Wolfie's weathered face were deep and shadowy in the dusky room. "Then he died, and I was left wondering if his crazy story was true."

Penelope braced herself for the question. "How did he

die, grandpa?"

Wolfie paused. "Bertram was hit by lightning. Right outside of this cabin."

A chill ran through Penelope's body and she remembered the tree falling inches from her face. "I never knew," she murmured.

"I chose not to tell you. I didn't want to scare you. I never told your mother, either. I wanted to believe that Bertram's theory was crazy. I thought never mentioning it would mean protecting you. I locked up his cabin and forbade you all to enter and put the past behind me." Wolfie was silent, considering what to say next. "But then your mother..."

The icy feeling in Penelope's bones deepened. "What." She gripped Wolfie's forearm. "What."

"It's true, what I told you and Veronica, that your mother died in an accident when you were very small. And it's also true that we never knew for sure what happened that day." Wolfie's face was pinched. "But there were things I didn't tell you. As far as the authorities could discern, your mother was swept into the sea. She was at the Old Docks, which is the same place that Bertram claimed to have seen the cursed starfish.

"After your mother died, I went down to the Old Docks. But I didn't see anything out of the ordinary. There was a starfish, but it didn't look anything like this one that Bertram had painted on his wall. It looked ordinary to me." Wolfie shrugged. "I still hoped that Bertram was wrong about the whole thing, that your mother's death was a freak accident. I wanted to forget about it all. I threw myself into the business of raising you and your sister, and hoped I'd never hear about a cursed starfish again."

Penelope gazed at the starfish on the wall. Raindrops hammered the roof overhead, and wind pushed at the fragile old cabin's walls.

Wolfie squeezed her chilled fingers. "There's something else you should see."

He swung the flashlight to the right and the beam tracked towards the corner of the room. There, tucked into the shadows, were words and numbers. Penelope scanned them, reading aloud. "'Otto 1900. Alice 1920.' I don't understand," she said to Wolfie. "Who are Otto and Alice?"

His voice was heavy. "My father, and my sister."

"How did they die?"

"My father was lost at sea when I was very small, and my sister froze to death on the beach when she was only 19."

"Froze to death?" Penelope blurted. "On the Oregon Coast?"

Wolfie made his way to a rickety chair in the corner and lowered himself into it. "Most of my life, I believed those to be random accidents."

Penelope reeled with the tragedies Wolfie had carried by himself. "Now do you think their deaths had something to do with the starfish?"

"I don't know. I think that's what Bertram thought. He painted this and wrote their names on the wall before he died. I found it after he was gone."

Penelope considered the storms of the last two weeks,

and the tree that had fallen at her feet. Could these things truly be because of a haunted starfish? A creepy feeling washed over her again. "Let's get out of here, Grandpa."

The two walked into the cabin's main room, where opaque light poured through the old, dirty windows. Penelope could see that it was raining, and moved to pull her jacket hood up over her head so that they could go back home.

Wolfie reached for her. "I don't understand what is going on, but I can't lose you the way I lost my father, sister, uncle, and your mother. If Bertram's theory is correct, you have been cursed, and we have to protect you, and those around you."

Penelope was cold now, cold to her bones, and very scared. "What does that mean?"

Coming up the hill earlier, her grandfather had looked young and spritely. But now the lines on his face were deep in the low light and his whole body slumped with fatigue.

"You can't go back home. We have to get you out of Starfish Cove."

THURSDAY, JANUARY 7, 1999

9:30 P.M.

Skye had never been to Bertram's cabin. She'd never even been up on the north cliffs. She'd been told specifically not to go there. For that matter, she'd never even been told Bertram existed.

But she knew where the cabin was, at least vaguely, because she knew where the Starfish Cove Hotel had been. She'd seen historical photos of the hotel, and how it overlooked both the sea and the cove. But how would she get up there? The route from the beach up the cliffside was long ago eroded. If there were a trail, it would have to climb up from the east, on the other side of Lewis Creek upstream through the forest.

Skye didn't know where the trail was—if it even existed—let alone how to navigate the way in the dark and rain. But she didn't have a choice but to try to find out. Her family was at risk and it was because of her. She couldn't stay near them and continue to put them in danger. She had to follow the note-writer's directions and hope they would lead to answers.

Skye set out on foot from the house, heading east up Lewis Street. It was total dark, the kind of dark that made you think that the moon was not only obscured, maybe the moon didn't even exist anymore. The rain was light, especially compared to the last few days. But still, the droplets were cold on her cheeks and obscured her view of what lay ahead. She pulled her jacket tighter and forged ahead carefully. She didn't want to turn on the flashlight until she was well away from her own house, in case someone might catch sight of her sneaking away into the night.

As she trudged through the dark, Skye cosidered her predicament. She'd never considered herself a brave person. She didn't take risks; she did her homework. She didn't disobey her parents, and she certainly didn't take off in the dead of night to try to find an abandoned and possibly haunted cabin in the thick of the woods on a cliff. What would the cabin look like? She doubted it would look like Disneyland, lit up like a welcoming castle.

Lewis Creek cut to the north upstream of the bridge, which meant that just ahead, Skye would have to jog north a block to avoid it. As she approached, the splashing of the water grew louder. Images of Andrew in the creek flashed in her mind and her eyes strained into the darkness to see the water. Was the creek as high as before?

Skye stopped and looked over her shoulder. Two houses were behind her, on her left. Both looked dark and quiet. She reached into her bag for the flashlight and switched it on. The light glinted off of the wet street before her. She moved the beam forward until she could see the creek—it was very high, with roiling waves and a powerful current. But it hadn't breached its banks, or submerged the bridge.

Skye forced herself to go on. Upstream, the houses disappeared and the road narrowed. Darkness enveloped her and the forest loomed ahead. An instinct took hold and guided her way. The sense was like a memory, even when it couldn't have been. She sensed if not saw the woods around her. She tried to resist the fear of what was coming.

The starfish flashed into her mind, pulsing blue at its center. She pushed it from her mind. What was done was done. Right there, she was compelled to stop. Skye shone her flashlight into the salal and huckleberry to the left. There, in the dim light, a break in the shrubbery marked a trail. Summoning all of her bravery, Skye stepped off the road and into the woods.

The forest enveloped her. Beneath her feet, compacted ground. She climbed a narrow and muddy trail up a hill. The sounds of the creek grew more distant as the wind grew stronger, whipping the tops of the Douglas fir overhead. She burst from the forest to the cliff top where the wind screamed past her ears into the sky.

Skye walked to the edge of the cliff. The moon glinted through clouds, reflecting on the sea. Below was the outline of the Old Docks, and the white tips of waves as they slid up the beach. Beyond was Starfish Cove, in a sprinkling swath of lights. Her hometown looked placid and quiet, nothing like the violent upheaval of the last few days. She'd never seen the town like this, at night, from above, and it was so beautiful.

A harsh gust of wind pushed at her chest and a chill crept up her spine as she thought of her family back home in bed. She missed Andrew. Dark clouds slid over the moon, casting Starfish Cove in shadows again. Skye wheeled back from the cliff's edge and pressed along the cliff trail, carefully in the gloom and the wind. She came across a huge tree that lay fallen across the trail, and awkwardly climbed over the trunk.

As she did, her flashlight beam caught the outline of a structure tucked off of the trail to her right. She'd nearly passed it. The cabin was small, and dark, and ensconced in shadows. Skye took a few steps forward, studying the little house. The structure looked totally abandoned, and several of the windows were broken. The front steps were only halfway there, the middle section broken through.

Skye stood poised between the cliff and the cabin. *Seek answers at Bertram's cabin.* Her mind told her to turn away and run down the hill as fast as she could to her own safe house. Skye thought of the starfish. She thought about the lightning, and the windstorm, and the flooding creek. Skye pointed her flashlight on the front door of her great-uncle Bertram's cabin like a beacon. She moved across the clearing and put her foot on the first, creaky step.

THURSDAY, JANUARY 7, 1999
10:27 P.M.

The door to the cabin was unlocked. The knob was cold and loose in Skye's hand, and squeaked as she twisted it. Her heart pounded. What would she find behind the door? For all she knew, the creepy old place was inhabited with crazy hobos or a pack of goblins. She strained to listen for danger over the pounding in her head. The latch clicked. The door slid open smoothly. Inside, darkness. The smell of damp wood, fireplace soot and mildew.

Skye hesitated. She turned back the way she'd come, towards the sea. But what was there was nothing. The wind had quit abruptly, and the entire cliff had become enveloped in impenetrable fog. The dense fog moved across the lawn towards her, as if it were a living entity.

She couldn't see even as far as the spot in the clearing where she'd stood only moments ago. She wouldn't be able to find her way anywhere. In fog like this, her flashlight would be useless—she'd wander right off the cliff. She turned and peered into the dark unknown of the cabin. As the creeping fog reached her back, Skye stumbled through the open door towards whatever came next.

Her feet hit the floorboards with a jolt and she slid the flashlight beam around the room. The light illuminated a rickety chair in one corner, and a table in another. A large stone fireplace anchored the back wall. A small kitchen was tucked in the back corner of the cabin—an ancient stove, a white sink. The front door slid shut behind her, closing with a definitive click that made Skye jump out of her skin. She took a few breaths and contemplated her situation.

It was only now that she was inside that she wondered what she was supposed to do here. *Seek answers at Bertram's cabin.* She had. But now she wasn't sure why. What would she find here? A person or a thing? There wasn't much to see so far. No fortune teller spouting answers, no trunks full of secrets. Skye walked into the kitchen and peered around in the dark. She pulled open a cupboard door on rusty hinges and shone her beam inside. Nothing. The corners of the room held only dust. Out the window over the small table, her light disappeared into a bank of charcoal colored fog.

Skye moved to the fireplace and peered into the sooty dark hole. She sat on the hearth. The stone was cold and damp beneath her blue jeans, but it looked sturdier than the broken-down chair. A few stray pieces of firewood lay nearby, and she wondered why she hadn't brought any matches. Who knows how much good they would do anyway—the wood looked half-rotted.

Skye sat on the cold hearth, listening. After the last few days of clamoring weather, the silence of the fog was unsettling. Creaks and clicks came from the old cedar planks settling into the earth. If she missed Andrew so much right now, how could it feel to her mother to know she would never see her sister again? Skye shivered and wished for a blanket.

She placed her backpack on the hearth beside her like a cold and lumpy pillow, and lay down. Her 14th birthday was five days away. She didn't know where she'd be, or with whom. She pulled her hood tight over her head and tried not to think about starfish, strange notes, storms or things she couldn't know and couldn't control.

Soon, she fell asleep.

THURSDAY, JANUARY 7, 1999
11 P.M.

Penelope couldn't sleep. She sat in her blue armchair by the fire and thought. A fleece blanket tucked over her knees, and a cup of hot tea steamed in both hands. Out the window, where during the day she could see the flanks of Mt. Hood, was now only darkness and quiet.

Sitting and thinking, Penelope always had plenty of time for that. She'd been living alone in this cabin on the mountain for nearly 14 years, and solitude and the companionship of her own mind were familiar conditions. But the last few days had been something else altogether. It wasn't thinking she was doing so much as worrying. Stewing. And struggling to know things she couldn't possibly know. Like what was happening 140 miles away. Who had seen the starfish. If her family was okay.

"What do you think, Charlie?" she asked aloud. Penelope did have her precious cat, and she spoke out loud to him more often than was probably advisable.

"Meow," said Charlie. The ginger cat sometimes answered her, but he wasn't always particularly clear in his messaging.

Penelope gave him a pat. "I figured that's what you'd say."

She tried not to fret. Images of the storms of 1985 had raged in her mind for days. Rarely a day went by that she didn't think of those weeks so long ago. Those storms changed her life forever. But during the last few days, she'd thought of little else. On Tuesday, the weather had been sudden and awful. A thunderstorm had moved up the mountain, violent and scary. It settled over her cabin, rain pounding at the rooftop and thunder shaking the walls. Spikes of lightning shot through the sky. Penelope was unsettled, with an all-too-familiar sense of unease.

That night, she'd switched on her ancient television, which received one channel from Portland via antenna. The news reporter talked over a video clip of lightning bolts striking the ocean. The hair stood up on the back of her neck. She knew that beach. A chill settled over her and she kept her eyes glued to the set. Weather in the rest of Oregon was calm, the reporter said, even as a storm raged over her head. Penelope could feel what was coming in her bones.

She drove into Rhododendron at dawn and mailed the first letter. That night's footage—the roof ripped off the golf course clubhouse. The next day, the raging creek, and the footage of Andrew and Skye on the beach after the flood. The first time she'd seen either of their faces in 14 years, since they were tiny children. She was captivated by their beauty and familiarity, even as she knew they were in deep trouble.

The next morning, she'd mailed the second letter.

Penelope's focus came back to the fire and the cozy room. This had been her home since Wolfie had driven her here that January day in 1985. The cabin had belonged to a friend of his, and the transaction was quick. In a day, decisions were made that changed everything. She'd barely had time to digest what was happening.

But how could she argue with Wolfie? He was so scared. Scared for Penelope, scared for Veronica and her family, scared for himself and the possibility of facing more loss. The only solution he could see was to hide her here on Mt. Hood, far away from the starfish and any harm to befall them all.

Penelope knew it had been a risk and a leap of faith to send the letters to Skye. She had made the decision in a hurry, by elimination and hunch. She needed to warn someone. She couldn't send word to Veronica—she knew her sister, and a mysterious letter about a curse would dig up the past and terrify her. If Penelope sent the letters to David, he would likely dismiss it, or hide it, to protect Veronica.

Ideally, the letters would reach the person who had seen the starfish. Penelope had no way of knowing who that person was. And yet, she had a hunch. If the starfish intended to curse her sister Veronica, that would've happened long ago. Penelope had only met her niece once before the tree had fallen and everything in her life changed. She'd held that tiny baby girl in her arms at the hospital as the storm raged outside the window, and felt a bond with her. It was a different feeling than she'd had with Andrew, her nephew. She adored him, but he was like a small alien in his loud, boy ways. Skye looked at Penelope with her blue eyes, as wind howled and rain pounded outside, and Penelope felt a chill. She couldn't explain it at the time. The following day, the tree had fallen, and by the end of the next day, Penelope had left Starfish Cove forever.

Charlie had settled by the fire, his head tucked into his arms in contentment. It was the dead of night and Penelope should get to bed. She sighed and sipped her tea, absentmindedly tugging at a strand of her hair. She thought of Andrew and Skye on television the other day, and how Skye lay her head on her brother's chest. Penelope remembered being on the verge of 14—feeling vulnerable while at the same time full of a strange new strength.

Penelope thought about the third letter, the one that she'd mailed to Skye from Rhododendron this morning. She hoped it wasn't too late. She recalled the object that she'd tucked inside. She could only hope that the letter reached her niece, and that Skye would follow the directions Penelope had given her.

FRIDAY, JANUARY 8, 1999
6:21 A.M.

Skye awoke to the sound of rain on the cabin roof. Water droplets drummed against the shakes with a steady patter. Somewhere inside the cabin, a slow, cadenced drip fell. She kept her eyes shut, listening to the rain. If she didn't open her eyes, she could pretend she was in her own bed in her own house. But the hard stone under her and the cold damp air surrounding her made it clear she wasn't in her own room, not even close.

Skye forced open one eye, then the other. She took a deep breath and sat up, her whole body aching from the night on the hearth. A morning light streamed through the dingy windows, illuminating what hadn't been clear in the dim beam of the flashlight the night before. The chair in the corner was a faded blue. The table only had three legs—its fourth leg lay on the floor, as if it had one day become too tired to hold the table up and decided to lie down for a nap. The floorboards were wide and dark, worn smooth and covered in a layer of dirt.

The place was shabby, and entirely abandoned, but

it wasn't as ominous as it had been last night. She could imagine that at one time, this little cabin on the cliff overlooking the sea might have been the nicest place in the world.

Skye rose and crossed to the front of the room. She yawned, tucked her hands into the pocket of her hoodie, and peered out of the small window. A gnarled old apple tree grew in the yard. The eerie fog of last night was gone. A light rain fell; through the mist, the steel-tinted ocean was visible beyond the edge of the cliff. From this vantage point, the sky and the sea looked continuous, as if together they were one vertical sheet of blue-tinged-grey.

She watched the far-away waves rise and fall, the water surging into the sky and then the sky chasing it back down again. What was happening back home with her family? How would they feel to awaken and find her gone? Confused. Scared. Anxious. They would go looking for her. She hated to think of how they would worry, but no amount of worry was as bad as the danger she put them in. She needed to keep herself, and the curse, as far away from her family as possible. Skye didn't understand why she had been sent to this cabin, or who sent her, but she hoped at least her family was safe for now.

Time for action, whatever that meant. She grabbed her backpack and dug out the letters and a granola bar. While she read and reread the messages, she munched on the crunchy peanut butter snack.

She who saw the glow is the center of the storms. Seek answers at Bertram's cabin.

The handwriting was neat. She didn't recognize it. She

sighed and shoved the letter back in her backpack. *Okay, mysterious note writer. I'm here! What now?*

She couldn't wait here forever. She didn't have enough granola bars. There must be something she was missing. Skye moved into the kitchen, intending to root around in the cupboards, when she saw a closed door on the room's north wall. The door was painted a faded blue and had an intricate brass doorknob. A sensation passed through her. The thought of opening that door made her as nervous as entering the cabin in the first place. Maybe this was where the goblins were, or the hobos.

But this was no time for fear. The doorknob was cold against her fingertips. She jerked her fingers back and zipped around the corner, grabbing her flashlight before returning to the door and throwing it open before she had time to think about what would happen next.

The room was empty. No hobos, no goblins, not even any furniture. But what *was* there took her breath away. Stretching across the back wall, lit by milky rays of sun streaming through a window, was a starfish. The figure was much bigger than life, done in mottled paint. The art was faded, but the shape was as plain as day.

Skye gazed in awe. It was a starfish, for sure, but not just any starfish. Most of the painting was a brownish-orange, but the center of the animal was a cerulean shade of blue dotted with little silver splotches. This was her starfish. The starfish at the center of the curse.

Now she knew why she was here. She put her hand on the wall, right over the blue patch in the starfish's center.

"Hey, guy," she whispered. "Who made you? And

what do you have to tell me?"

She brushed her hand across the surface of the painting, feeling the rough plaster beneath her palm, tracing the starfish's limbs. As she drew her hand over the fifth leg, she caught sight of words to the right of the starfish. A list. The artist used black paint for this part of the job, each word carefully inscribed atop the other.

Skye quickly scanned the names and numbers.

Otto 1900

Alice 1920

Bertram 1945

Heather 1962

Penelope 1985

101 - 26 – 84 – 26 - 18 - 1828 - 1825 – 100 – END

Skye recognized a couple of these names. Bertram was her great-uncle who had lived in this cabin and apparently been struck dead by lightning. Penelope was her aunt, gone days after Skye was born in 1985. The year 1962 was two years after Veronica and Penelope were born—was Heather their mother, who they had lost when they were so young?

She didn't know who Alice and Otto were. The dates by their names meant that they had lived long ago. This list was the names of the Dead Beckendorfs. It had to be. Was it also those cursed by the starfish?

Skye wondered who had painted the names and dates

on the wall. This was Bertram's cabin, but he couldn't have written his own name, not if this was a list of the dead. And there were names that came after his. Someone had been here more recently than Bertram's death. What were the numbers under the names?

If Skye was meant to see this painting, if this was the reason the note writer sent her to this cabin, that goal had been achieved. But she was still baffled. She had no idea what any of this meant.

Skye rested her hand on the starfish's center. *What now?* She had more questions than ever before.

FRIDAY, JANUARY 8, 1999

2:07 P.M.

Skye paced and thought. Time was eternity when all she had to do was worry. There was nothing to do in the small cabin, but she couldn't focus anyway. Her mind spun with possibilities, never settling on any solution. She didn't know what the answers were—she barely understood the questions.

She thought about her family a lot. *Was coming here the right thing to do?* Was it better to stay near and put the ones she loved at risk or leave and cause them worry?

Outside, the weather had taken a turn. The wind howled even more insistently than the night before. Up on the cliff, even in the shelter of the cabin, Skye felt closer to the weather, more vulnerable, as if she was one with the sky, for better or worse. The wind sucked over the rooftop and whistled down the chimney, and the old cabin walls swayed and creaked in response.

Skye loved the weather, and had always treated it with endless curiosity. But now that interest was tinged with fear. Weather was different when it turned destructive.

And now she was to believe she was responsible? That made her afraid to even think about the weather.

Skye contemplated running back down the woodsy trail and asking for help. Instead, she returned to Wolfie's bedroom and sat on the floor. She looked at the starfish painting for a long time, waiting for insight. Nothing came. She left the room and closed the door. She returned to her place at the hearth and waited. For what, she had no idea. She ate her second granola bar at what she figured was around noon. She wasn't hungry, but her stomach had never been emptier.

After a while, Skye lay her head down on her backpack and closed her eyes. She meant only to rest for a moment, but soon she'd slipped into sleep.

The cabin door flew open and a figure burst into the room, bringing in a surge of wind and rain. Skye blasted off of the hearth in a panic, braced for attack.

"Stormy!" said Andrew with relief, crossing the room and throwing his arms around his sister. Skye sunk into her brother's chest, so grateful to see him she didn't mind her face pressing into the wet folds of his rain jacket. He was out of breath and she imagined him climbing the cliff trail, making the same journey she had the night before.

Skye was so relieved that she almost forgot her predicament. She was about to ask her brother how he had found her, but then she remembered. It didn't matter how Andrew had found her, only that he should leave immediately. Andrew wasn't safe as long as he was near her.

Skye pushed hard at Andrew's chest with both hands. "You shouldn't have come here."

Andrew took a step back, shocked and confused. "Why not?"

"I'll put you in danger." Skye was upset now. The tears were coming and she crossed her arms tight across her middle. "Everything is my fault. The traffic light, the whirlwind, the windstorm—you almost drowning in the creek! All of it is because of me."

Andrew gave a sharp exhale. "How is that possible? First, you thought the storms were because of Mom, and now they are because of you?" His voice was loud, his face red and glistening from the rain.

"But it really is me." It was surreal to say it out loud. "I was wrong about Mom. It's my fault. I'm the one who saw the starfish. I am the center of the storms."

Skye focused on the planks of Douglas fir beneath her feet. She was dizzy and sick. She waited for Andrew to tell her she was crazy, to continue to rail at her in disbelief. But her brother said, "So it's true."

Skye studied Andrew's face. She had many questions, but she chose one. "How did you know I was here?"

"Mr. Terwilliger."

Now it was Skye's turn to be surprised. "Our gym teacher?"

Andrew smiled. "I guess we both have a few things to explain."

Skye swept her hand towards the hearth. "Come into my office. I don't suppose you brought any matches and firewood?"

Andrew sat next to Skye and took in the shabby room. "So this is where uncle Bertram lived."

"And died. He was hit by lightning, right out front."

Andrew cringed. "So we finally learned how one of The Dead Beckendorfs became dead."

He took a deep breath. "Okay—do you remember, the day the roof blew off the clubhouse, that strange comment Mr. Terwilliger made after we snuck back into the school? He said something about how we should know to be careful about the weather in Starfish Cove."

"I remember," Skye said. "It didn't make any sense."

"When I realized you were gone this morning, with everything that's been going on—I was worried. I told Mom and Dad you'd left early to meet up with Ashley, and then I tried to figure out where you'd gone."

Andrew's knee bobbed up and down as his story picked up pace. "I looked for you along the creek, and then at the beach, but you weren't anywhere and the weather was crap so I doubted you were outside anyway. I went to the school to look for you and that's when I remembered Mr. Terwilliger's comment. I found him in the gym."

Andrew's words mixed with the sounds of the rain. "At first, he didn't want to tell me. Did you know that Mr. Terwilliger used to work with Mom's grandfather, Wolfie?"

Skye let out a laugh. "How would I know that? No one tells us anything."

"Wolfie Beckendorf was Mr. Terwilliger's mentor at the high school. Wolfie retired ages ago, but he and Mr. Terwilliger stayed close. Right before Wolfie died, he

141

told Mr. Terwilliger that he believed his family had been afflicted with a curse. Wolfie swore he keep the secret, but told him that if anything ever happened to a Beckendorf, Bertram's old cabin would reveal answers. Mr. Terwilliger said that if you were missing, I should check here."

Skye tried to put this new information together with what she already knew. *Wolfie must have written those names on the wall,* Skye thought. *Was Mr. Terwilliger the one who had written her the letters?*

"But how did *you* end up here?" Andrew asked.

Skye dug the letters out of her backpack and handed them to Andrew. He read each. Then he handed them back to her and reached his hand into his own pocket. When he pulled it out again, he held an envelope.

Skye Clancy, it read on the outside, in the same neat handwriting as the other letters, followed by their address. Portland, Oregon postmark. In the corner, a Christmas stamp. Skye snatched the letter out of her brother's hands and clutched it to her chest, protective and scared at the same time.

Andrew didn't protest. "I opened it already. This morning. I'm sorry. I thought whatever was in there might give me a clue to where you'd gone."

He paused, regarding the letter in her hands. "But what's in there didn't tell me anything. All it did was creep me out." He shrugged. "Even after seeing your other two letters, I don't get it."

Skye opened the envelope and slipped her fingers inside. When she withdrew them, she held a folded map. She unfolded the paper until a large sheet spread in her lap. The map was of the state of Oregon. She knew this shape well. She recognized the Pacific coastline to the west, the jagged edge that followed the Columbia River upriver to the east, the ridge of the Cascade Range as it ran north to south down the center of the state. She spotted the big star on the Columbia that marked Portland, and the tiny indent in the coastline that marked Starfish Cove. The map was very detailed, with many roads and terrain defined with various colors.

Skye's eyes traveled to the top of the map. Across the upper margin, written in the handwriting of Skye's personal messenger, was this:

You must come to me.

FRIDAY, JANUARY 8, 1999

3:07 P.M.

"See." Andrew pointed at the words on the map. "Creepy."

Skye considered the words. *You must come to me.*

She didn't know why, but these words did not frighten her. "I think whoever is sending these messages is on our side. I think we need to trust them."

"Okay." Andrew was dubious. "But even if we trust them—how do we find them?" He gestured at the map again. "There aren't any directions on there."

"That's true," Skye mused. There weren't any other markings on the map besides the words at the top. She turned the map over in her hands, searching for more writing, drawings added to the map's topography, something to explain what she should do.

Nothing.

She was puzzled. The letter writer probably wasn't Mr. Terwilliger, after all. He wouldn't need to send letters in the mail or give her a map of the entire state to get her attention. All he had to do was ask her to stay late for gym.

Whoever it was, he or she was somewhere in Oregon. But where? It was a big state. Without directions, how could she find them? And *should* she find them? What if this was all a freakish trap?

No, she thought. *I think this person means well.*

Whoever it was knew about her, knew where she lived, seemed to know a lot about her family history and had taken the effort to warn her about the curse. The letter writer knew about this cabin, too—Skye had been sent here, where she had found the starfish painting.

The painting.

Skye leapt from the hearth, carrying the map with her. Andrew followed behind. She threw open the door with the brass knob and looked at the wall, the map still clutched in her hand.

Andrew pulled up behind her and then stopped short. "Holy whoa," he said.

She let her brother take in the painting. The afternoon light shone brighter through the window than earlier in the day, illuminating the enormous starfish's eerie blue center.

Skye considered the starfish as well, mulling over her theory as the wind roared over the rooftop and rattled the old pane in the bedroom window.

She approached the words and numbers painted on the wall. Her eyes flicked back and forth between the wall and the map in her hand several times before she made her decision.

"I know where we're going," Skye said. She pointed at the numbers, reading them aloud:

"101 - 26 – 84 – 26 - 18 - 1828 - 1825 – 100 – END," she said. "These are road numbers."

Skye faced her brother, who was looking at her like she was a brand new person. "These numbers correlate with Oregon highways."

"See." Skye sank to her knees and smoothed the map flat on the dusty fir floorboards. She pointed at Starfish Cove. "We're on Highway 101—that's the first number."

She ran her finger up the left side of the map, along the coast highway. "101 runs into 26 here, by Seaside, and heads west to Portland." As she dragged her finger across the map, she looked to the wall and back, scanning each crossroad in search of the next number. Andrew stood over her, watching curiously.

"26 continues through Portland as I-84 and then keeps going to Mt. Hood." Skye's finger slowed as she traced across the paper, tracking road numbers. "Here." She poised her finger on the map along Highway 26 between Welches and Rhododendron. "26 doesn't meet 1828 until way over here, on the way to Mt. Hood."

Skye crouched over the map, peering in the half-light at the small lines that traversed the paper. "It's a Forest Service road that heads into the woods. It's also called Lolo Pass Road. Then what…it winds around a little bit and forks onto 1825."

"This is why this map is so big," she said. "Otherwise it wouldn't show these tiny roads. It looks like 100 peters out on the flanks of Mt. Hood. I guess that's what "End" means?"

She took another second to be sure and then jabbed at

the map. "There." Skye planted her forefinger on a green patch of map, just west of the peak of the mountain.

She sat back on her heels and looked up at her brother. Andrew was dazed. Skye had never been more certain about anything. "Andrew," she announced. "We have to go there."

Andrew took his time. "Nice detective work, Stormy. I'm impressed." Then he threw his arms in the air. "But you're completely insane!" His voice rose and his eyes went wild. "You want us to drive halfway across the state of Oregon, up a mountain, into the middle of nowhere, in January—to find what? We don't even know what's there! We have no idea! And here's a better question—*who* is there?"

Skye gazed at the starfish on the wall. "I don't know."

"And who the heck are *those* people?" Andrew's voice competed with the howling wind as he gestured at the list of names on the wall.

Skye smiled at her brother. "Andrew, those are the Dead Beckendorfs. Our family. They were killed by this curse, apparently. If we don't want to join them, we have to follow these directions. We need to find what is at the end of the road. We have to stop the curse."

Andrew looked at her like she'd lost her mind. Skye was not to be deterred. "Where's the Honda?"

"At the bottom of the trail," Andrew said weakly. "I parked it at the top of Pine Street, kind of in the bushes so no one would see it."

"Okay, good." Skye rose and crossed the room to the starfish on the wall, placing her hand on his belly one more time, as if thanking the image or asking one last question or saying goodbye, she wasn't sure.

"Stormy." Andrew's voice was tinged with doubt. "I've never been to Mt. Hood."

"Me either."

His face was pale. "I've never driven by myself *outside of this county*. I've only had a driver's license for four months."

"I know."

"This is crazy."

"True," said Skye.

Andrew watched the rain lashing at the glass. "The future of all Beckendorf descendants is at stake?"

"I think so?" Skye made an exaggerated shrug.

"Well, then. Let's go."

FRIDAY, JANUARY 8, 1999
3:54 P.M.

Skye and Andrew recorded the numbers from the wall, tucked the map into Skye's backpack with the other two letters, latched the door to their great-uncle's cabin and ventured outside under a darkening late afternoon sky. The wind whipped around them in tiny tornadoes and the rain hammered on their heads as they crossed the clearing towards the cliff.

At the edge, Skye paused. Overhead, a gargantuan cloud loomed. Below, waves surged. Water slammed into the rocky base of the cliff, pushing up the face like the fingers of a vicious sea monster reaching for Andrew and Skye before crashing down violently to rejoin the water below.

A week ago, Skye had considered the weather to be fascinating but utterly beyond her control. It was something to be interpreted, like Jerry did, like a big mystery to solve every single day.

In the last week, things had changed. She had underestimated the wrath of the sky. She was powerless to its destruction and frightened of her role in it. For a time, she had wanted nothing to do with the weather ever again.

But now, on the cliff overlooking the churning maelstrom, Skye was filled with a sense of purpose. She would never think of the weather in the same way again. If the storms of the past week were truly related to a curse, and she had the power to do something about that, then of course, she must do it. A flash of excitement shot through her.

Andrew stood beside her, his arms wrapped around his middle, and his face scrunched up against the storm. He seemed to understand that she needed a moment to take in the wild scene one last time before they went, and waited several minutes before he finally took her elbow. "Okay," he said. "We're getting annihilated out here, and it's getting late."

The Clancy siblings descended the cliff trail through the forest down to the creek. The sky delivered more light than when Stormy had come up to the cabin in the night, and surrounding her were the looming, majestic trees, glossy salal, and holly green boxwood. The wind off of the creek below was cold and crisp, while the wind from the ocean behind them was warm and salty. The two forces swirled together, filling Skye with a burgeoning strength.

Andrew led with a determined gait. They bolted down the trail, exchanging no words. At the trail end, Andrew peered down the road. No one was around. The Honda was parked between the end of the road and the creek, tucked into shrubbery. They jumped inside.

The engine on the old car wearily chugged to life, and

Skye contemplated what was next. She could only assume that soon, if not already, her parents would figure out their children had gone missing. She knew there was no way on this planet David and Veronica would ever allow Skye and Andrew to drive to Mt. Hood on their own, let alone to visit a mysterious stranger. Which meant there was no way they could let them in on their plans.

But how would they get out of town unnoticed? Now wasn't a good time to get discovered by an overly helpful citizen. And it wasn't like this was a massive town in which they could get lost in the crowd. Everyone knew everyone in Starfish Cove, and there was only one way out of town.

Andrew was reading her mind. "We need the cloak of invisibility. You got that? Does that come with the starfish curse?"

Skye raised one eyebrow. "Not that I'm aware of."

"Then I guess we're relying on our wits—which, speaking from a personal standpoint, are questionable. So possibly we're relying on the only thing I've ever been able to hope for instead of wits—which is dumb luck."

"Right," Skye said. "It's worked for you before."

"So true!" Andrew seemed giddy. "Even Lucy went out with me for a while."

Skye threw a hand up dismissively. "She was worthless."

"Also true." Andrew didn't sound convinced. "But what if she's the only girl who will ever go out with me?"

"That's not what's going to happen. You're a catch. Think about your killer waffle making skills."

Andrew considered that as he backed the car, wheeling

151

it around to face west. Skye pulled the map from her backpack, folded it in half with the western half up, and spread it in her lap. "Let's get this road trip started," said Skye. "We have a stranger to meet!"

She turned to her brother, putting on a serious face. "But first, I wasn't honest with you. I do have the cloak of invisibility."

Andrew gaped. "Seriously?"

"No. Got you."

"Dang it! That would have been cool."

Andrew pulled away from the salal and flipped the wipers on high. "We'll be avoiding Main Street for obvious reasons. We need to cut down Lewis and sneak around the back way to Coast to get to 101."

He maneuvered the car down the narrow road to the south. As they approached the bridge, Skye held her breath. Her brother had crossed that bridge for the first time since the accident to find her. He had come anyway, with that raging creek still churning in his recent memory.

Now, Skye half-expected Andrew to hesitate before crossing. The bridge surface glistened with a sheen of water in the dimming daylight. Two gulls stood on the surface like statues. Skye looked at her brother. His fingers gripped the wheel. He pressed his feet to the floorboards and blasted the Honda across the bridge. The birds took flight in a flutter and screech.

As they traveled down Clark Street, Skye sank a little lower in her seat, pulling her hood over her head. Halfway up the first block, a dog ran into the street. Andrew kept steadily on and the dog slipped behind the car as the front door opened on the house to their right. "That was close."

The rain, for once, was on their side. In this weather, most people weren't outside, and the car's silver paint job blended with the falling rain. Andrew and Skye made it the three blocks to the end of the street without any interference, but the real test was still to come. The creek and the cliffs created natural barriers, and there was only one road out of Starfish Cove. Coast Avenue was the busiest road in town for that reason. If they were going to encounter someone they knew, it would be there.

Andrew made the left. From here, they had to navigate another four blocks west and make the turn left onto 101 to head north out of town. Four blocks, home to mostly businesses. They motored past the hardware store on the right, and then the grocery and real estate office. On the left was a clothing store and a take-out sandwich shop. The biggest building on the street was the public library, at the top of the road on the right, nearly to the highway. Once they passed the library, they were home-free.

The square brick building was coming up ahead. Andrew was rock solid, navigating the Honda steadily. Skye slid her eyes right, scanning the front of the library. She peered into the bank of windows facing the street, hoping no one she knew was behind the glass.

Just as the library skimmed out of view, Skye caught a flash of movement. The library doors blasted open. A person came flying out of the building, setting forth in a dead run towards the Honda.

"Andrew!" Skye cried out, but it was too late.

FRIDAY, JANUARY 8, 1999
4:36 P.M.

Andrew turned to see what Skye shouted about. He urged the Honda on, but the person running was surprisingly fast and reached the car on foot past the library. She banged on the side door, yelling like a banshee.

Andrew slowed down but didn't stop. Skye rolled down her window and poked her face out into the rain. "Ashley! Calm down! You're totally freaking out."

"Where have you been?" Ashley was frantic. "Where are you going? You've been missing all day!" She had one hand on the door and galloped alongside the car like a sideways pony.

"Go back to the sidewalk!" Skye demanded. "You're going to get your toes run over!"

"What do I do?" said Andrew, who had eased off the accelerator, frozen in indecision.

Skye was torn. They couldn't stop—they needed to get out of town as quickly as possible. But they couldn't go on with Ashley stuck to the side of the Honda. Anyway, she was making such a ruckus that pretty soon the whole town would be following them like a giant chaos parade.

"Why won't you tell me what's going on?" Ashley's face was red from exertion and wetter by the minute. Her curly hair bounced wildly as she tried to keep up.

Skye made a decision. "Andrew, stop."

Andrew slowed to a stop in the middle of the street.

Skye commanded, "Ashley, get in. Quickly!"

Ashley tugged open the Honda's back door and practically fell inside, bringing the fresh smell of rain mixed with wet cotton and hairspray with her.

"Andrew, go," said Skye.

Andrew obediently pushed at the accelerator, but before he returned his eyes to the road, he shot his sister a questioning look.

Skye shrugged. "She saw us. She saw us and she saw which way we were going. We have to take her with us."

Andrew nodded and made the left turn onto Highway 101. He accelerated on the glistening highway and the trees whipped past in a blur of green.

"Take me where?" Ashley asked.

"Mt. Hood," Skye replied. "Basically."

"Mt. Hood...BASICALLY?" Ashley's voice rose an octave.

Skye spun around and locked eyes with her friend. If Skye had her way, Ashley wouldn't even be in this car. Having Ashley along made things more complicated, not to mention that as far as Skye knew everyone around her was in danger.

They stared at each other in standoff. Skye had never

been so conflicted in her life, caught between concern and frustration, and as for Ashley, she had rain, worry and confusion all over her face.

Skye took a deep breath. "I'm sorry I yelled at you, Ash."

"It's okay," Ashley relented.

"There's a lot going on this week," said Skye, lamely.

"I understand," said Ashley, adding in confusion, "Kind of."

"And I'm sorry we tried to run you over. And kidnapped you. Basically." She burst into a nervous giggle, brimming with all of the tension of the past 24 hours.

Ashley snorted. "No worries. I was totally thinking about going to Mt. Hood today anyway."

Skye regarded her brother, who looked like the getaway driver of the year with one hand slung casually over the steering wheel. There were no other cars in sight, only the wide-open highway in front of them, black like a stone that had been dipped in water. To the west, the sky and the sun set blue and pink respectively through the rainstorm.

"Hey, Ashley," said Andrew, speaking for the first time since the library. "Welcome aboard. Did you bring the sandwiches?"

Ashley released a mirthful laugh. "I didn't get the memo. I didn't even grab my backpack. I saw you guys drive by and ran out the door like a crazy person. My mom is probably wondering where I went."

"Your mom was with you at the library?" Andrew asked.

"Yeah, researching *your* family! She figured out that *you* are the Becken-whoevers and she's on a mad hunt to learn what happened to your mom's sister and your grandpa wolf-something and your great-aunt somebody."

Ashley shifted, pulling off her wet jacket. "She and Jerry were rooting around in the newspaper archives, but I got bored. That's the only way I saw you—I was staring out the front windows waiting for everyone to be done with mystery science theater."

Skye absorbed this news. "Well. Andrew and I have a teeny idea about what happened to all of the Becken-whoevers. But it'll probably sound a little bit nuts."

"I love nuts," said Ashley.

"There's a curse," said Skye. "It has to do with a starfish. I saw the starfish, which means I have been stricken with the curse. As long as you are near me, you are in danger. We're using a special map to make our way to Mt. Hood to meet a mysterious stranger, figure out how to reverse the curse, and save our family and possibly Starfish Cove, too."

"Oh, good," said Ashley. "That all sounds perfectly reasonable, and like lots of fun."

The trio slipped into silence again, watching the scenery pass by. Glimpses of the ocean appeared in the twilight as the car wound over the hilly landscape. Highway 101 was famously scenic, snaking along the ocean, sometimes cresting cliffs that hung right over the sea. The surf tonight was boisterous waves tinted with the last light.

Skye spotted the highway sign warning of the upcoming fork in the road. Continue north on Highway 101 or veer west towards Portland on Highway 26. She pointed at the sign, and Andrew nodded, steering the car in a wide arc at the exchange.

Andrew seemed to relax even more now that they were on the second leg of their journey. The map did indeed match up to the highway numbers, at least so far. Andrew bumped the heater up and settled into a steady 55 miles per hour, per the speed limit. Soon, a green highway sign appeared.

Nehebo 10 miles
Portland 70 miles.

Skye suddenly had a question. "Andrew, how much gas do we have?"

He glanced down at the gauge. "About none."

FRIDAY, JANUARY 8, 1999

5:16 P.M.

Skye shot Andrew a wide-eyed look. "Seriously? We're out of gas?"

He flopped a hand in the air in exasperation. "I don't get paid from the Oyster until Fridays! I never fill the gas tank until after that. I don't drive that far usually. It's not like I burn much gas circumnavigating the entire one square mile throbbing metropolis of Starfish Cove."

The Honda had begun to ascend the hills east of the coastline. The Oregon Coast Range was nothing compared to the Cascade Range, which ran down the center of the state and rose to over 10,000 feet. Here, closer to the ocean, the mountains were modest.

Still, Skye knew from previous trips to Portland with her family that the roads over the range were winding and steep in places. Conditions were wet and could snow under the right circumstances. The forest was thick and impenetrable on either side of the highway, and rarely interrupted by signs of civilization of any kind. There wasn't much of anything out here—like gas stations.

"Andrew," pleaded Skye. "How much gas, really? Do we have enough to get over the mountain?"

Andrew looked at the dashboard. "Looks like less than a quarter-tank."

"Will that get us to the valley?"

"I don't know," Andrew shrugged. "I've never driven to the valley."

The Honda cruised on easily, showing no signs of suddenly sputtering to a stop. But how would you know? Skye had never been in a car that had run out of gas before.

"Well, what do we do? Do we have to turn around and go back?"

"I don't know."

"How far to the next gas station?"

"I don't know."

"Do you even have any money?"

"That is doubtful."

"Andrew, you're killing me right now!" Skye was starting to sweat. "How are we supposed to buy gas, if we even find gas? I don't have any money! I have a backpack, a map and a raincoat. And what about food? I'm starving. All I've had to eat since I left home last night is two granola bars."

Andrew was silent, keeping his eyes on the road as it wound around a long ascending corner.

"Seriously, Andrew! You are so irresponsible!" Skye was yelling now. She knew she was losing it but she couldn't help it. They were in the middle of the woods and she was hungry and it was getting dark and they didn't even know where they were going and they would need gas to figure that out. Her eye twitched and she struggled to hold it together.

"I'm irresponsible?" Andrew erupted. "C'mon, bro. The only reason we ran away from home and are driving to freaking Mt. Hood is because of you. I didn't know I was in charge of bringing the money and food for our fugitive escape."

"I'm sorry, okay! I didn't mean to get cursed." Skye's voice ricocheted around the car. "I don't know what to do. I'm doing the best I can considering I have apparently been afflicted with a freaking starfish curse!"

Andrew gripped the steering wheel and glared at the highway. Then a gurgle came from low inside of him. Her brother's face contorted in a struggle to keep a straight face. Next, a laugh spurted out of his lips. Then an outright guffaw.

Skye glowered at him.

"You have a *freaking starfish curse,* Stormy," Andrew managed. "It's a little bit new, kind of out-of-the-box. It's so 1999. We're *all* doing the best we can."

Skye laughed too. The car was warm inside now, and she was finally heating up and drying out after the cold night in the cabin and the hike through the woods. Out the window was a steep ravine, where a tiny stream flashed white in the waning light. The gorgeous Oregon woods flew past the window and the purpose of their journey reemerged. They didn't know what they were getting into. But they were in it together.

Their laughter settled and the lull of travel set in. A road sign warned cars to slow for an upcoming destination, and while Andrew did slow, there was nothing to note about Nehebo but a few darkened buildings. No gas, no food. The town, if you could call it that, came and went in the blink of an eye like so many other forgotten outposts.

Andrew sped up on the far side of the village. Fat drops of rain drowned out the sound of the engine. There was a rustling from the backseat. Skye startled out of her reverie—she had been so caught up in her argument with Andrew, she had forgotten about Ashley.

"Umm, Clancys?" Ashley said. "If you're done working out your drama, I have something to say."

Skye turned to face her friend. "Sorry, Ash. What is it?"

"I've got $25 in my pocket. My mom gave it to me to sign up for spring golf earlier this week. But I kept forgetting. I'm thinking gas and food are more important than me playing golf in the rain. Given the circumstances. And the golf course is kind of destroyed, also?"

Skye reached her hand back and found her friend's hand in the dark. "Ash. I'm glad you're here."

She turned to her brother. "How far until the next gas station?"

"Just around the bend," Andrew replied. "I'm sure of it."

35

FRIDAY, JANUARY 8, 1999
6:34 P.M.

The Honda rolled into the almost-town of Farmington on fumes. They had descended out of the forest and mountains into the fields of the Willamette Valley. Andrew spotted an Arco and navigated into a pump station, with the gas gauge needle wedged deeply into the red "empty" position and the gaslight glowing a golden orange.

"You may be cursed, Stormy, but someone looked out for us on this one." Andrew patted the Honda's dashboard. "Good job, little car."

Ashley dug the cash out of her jeans and handed Andrew $15 for gas, and the girls left the cozy interior of the car in exchange for the shock of a stormy world as they dashed towards the store. The rain continued to fall in sheets, cut sideways by a frigid wind.

The convenience store was small and smelled of gasoline and burnt coffee, and was stocked with the usual cheap snacks and sundries. A bored, pasty-faced clerk was behind the counter, with a television suspended from the ceiling over his head. As Skye and Ashley entered the store, the screen switched from an ad for an appliance store to a Portland News channel. An overly made-up woman with a serious look on her face said, "Wild storms continue on the northern Oregon coast today, putting residents at risk."

A video clip of Skye and Andrew on the beach the day before popped onto the screen, and Skye did a double take at her own scared and soggy self on TV.

Ashley stared at the television too, but forgot to quit walking and promptly ran right into a large cutout of a famous football player, marketing a brand of potato chips that everyone should buy before the Super Bowl. The cardboard cutout tumbled into the chips, which scattered chaotically across the floor.

"Sorry! Sorry! Sorry!" Ashley scooted around the room to collect the chips and right the face-planted football star as the clerk glared at them. Skye quickly grabbed three hot dogs from the heated case, nuts, juice and a Snickers bar, and paid the clerk as Ashley shoved all the chips back on to the display.

They hurried back to the car through the rain. Skye muttered, "Way to be low-profile."

Ashley threw her arms in the air. "I know—I'm not cut out to be a fugitive. You should have kidnapped someone else."

Andrew had the car running again. He pulled back onto Highway 26. "Now what?"

Skye dug the map out of her backpack and unfolded it on her lap while she munched on almonds. "We're on 26 for a while longer, but we have to get through the city."

"Right," said Andrew. "The next thing I get to do for

the first time—drive through a giant city in lots of traffic in the dark."

"And rain," added Skye.

Sunset was long gone. The highway ahead a sea of taillights, red and white flashing through the streaky windshield. The traffic grew thicker as they approached Portland. The lonely winding road of the Coast Range behind them seemed easy in hindsight. Big green signs indicating exits to come appeared overhead, the words and distances a blur of confusion.

Skye studied the map, trying to sort in her head the tangle of multi-colored threads circling the center dot of Portland.

"We want to stay on 26, but we need to get around the city," she said. "That's why there was that '84' in the middle of two 26s on the wall. 84 connects the 26s. So for now, follow the signs that lead to 84 East."

"Got it," said Andrew.

"Once we're on the other side of the city, we rejoin 26 and head up the mountain."

The noises and lights of the city were consuming. Andrew successfully wound the car through the twists and turns of the hills on the west side of Portland, and then through the tunnel into the city. They merged onto a highway that seemed wider than Starfish Cove. The little Honda joined five lanes of traffic surging around the city and then climbed a positively enormous bridge over the Willamette River, stretching into the sky in a looming arc.

Skye gaped at the flickering lights of the city below, reflected onto the river. Poised above the river on a concrete slab, it seemed as if they might drive right off into the sky. The wind pushed at the car and whipped over the Honda with a wailing screech. Skye held her breath as Andrew crossed two lanes, skimming across the wet surface of the bridge on the car's old tires.

A mewl of fear rose and Skye fought to suppress it— Andrew was doing such a good job and she didn't want to scare him. He merged the car to the far right, barely making the exit for 84. At the bottom of that ramp, they met another mass of cars, red brake lights blinking in the dark.

Andrew took a deep breath. His fingers were tight around the steering wheel and his eyes looked tired. "You're doing great," Skye said quietly.

"Yep, you are," said Ashley from the back seat.

84 spilled north and east, the traffic merging into another five-lane highway. Skye knew from the map that the massive Columbia River was to their left. She could imagine the huge body of water coursing through the gorge and back towards home, but it was thoroughly dark and she couldn't see a thing except for rain and taillights.

Highway 26
Mt. Hood
Next Right

The illuminated letters shone eerily bright and the words hit Skye with a shiver.

Andrew veered the Honda easily onto the off ramp. "To the mountain," he said, raising his fist in a half-hearted toast.

"To the mountain," Ashley said, and Skye repeated the words, too. She hoped that her voice didn't sound as hollow as it felt. She hoped her companions weren't bluffing like her, with the same fearful pit in their stomachs. If either of them had said "let's go home" right now, Skye would've agreed in an instant.

FRIDAY, JANUARY 8, 1999

7:28 P.M.

The road narrowed and climbed after the Honda left the freeway. Skye had been to Portland, but never beyond, never to the Cascades. Her parents had not shown the least bit of interest in the snowy mountains that ran through Oregon. Now, she inched up the flanks of Oregon's tallest mountain.

A massive Douglas fir forest closed around them, trunks flashing by in the Honda's headlights. The forest was similar to the one she knew at home, but these trees seemed more imposing. They were driving into the unknown. A chill seeped into the car as they climbed in elevation. Skye reached for the heater dial and flipped it to its highest setting.

They passed through small towns, a diner or a grocery store lit up here or there. The water that had been falling on the windshield for their entire journey began to change. Raindrops thickened and slid down the glass in slow motion, like silvery splotches of melting ice cream. Then the silver splotches turned to white, and stuck to the windshield like tiny cotton balls before the wipers swiped them away.

Skye was mesmerized. She'd never seen snow before. The falling flakes were so beautiful. But the sight infused her with dread. Snow meant cold and slick, and cold and slick meant bad roads. Andrew didn't know how to drive in *snow*.

As if he'd read her mind, he said, "How much further to our next turn?"

Skye returned to the map. "The last sign said Mt. Hood Village, which is here." She placed her finger on the map. "Road 18 is a few miles away. Maybe two or three."

Andrew cruised delicately through each bend as if he held his breath and willed the car to stay on the road. Skye honed in on the scene ahead. The snowflakes grew larger by the minute as they continued to ascend the mountain. The sign came up quickly.

"There," Skye said. "Turn here."

A large stone and wood installment that read "National Forest" marked the entrance to Road 18, Lolo Pass Road. The road was narrow with a layer of wet snow accumulated on the surface and more piled at the sides.

Skye peered through fat flakes of snow, trying to see what was coming next. Andrew pressed on, and the tires slipped beneath them as the Honda struggled to maintain traction. "Just keep going," Skye whispered, to convince herself as much as encourage her brother.

In the backseat, Ashley was silent. Skye turned; her friend was gazing out the window into the bleak winter darkness with a preoccupied focus. Ashley hated rain, wind and sand—how would she feel about snow, dark and mountains?

Skye pointed Andrew onto a slight right fork labeled 1828. They almost missed the right onto 1825 a couple of miles later—the snow came down hard now and the wipers fought to keep up. The road grew muckier and stickier with every half-mile. Andrew kept up a consistent pace even as the back wheels fishtailed behind them.

"I'm afraid to stop—we'll get stuck," he murmured.

They hadn't seen another car since 26. The forest road was dark and abandoned. If they got stuck, what would happen? They were utterly alone. No one knew where they were. Skye's heart beat fast.

Skye was worrying so much she nearly missed the turn to 100. The opening in the forest flashed in her peripheral vision, a dark sliver of a road to the left, overgrown on either side with brush.

"Andrew, there!" He spun the Honda into an arc on the snowy road. The car swung wildly and Skye hung on the dash as the car barely missed the trees at road's edge. They caught the turn but nearly crashed into the small brown post marked "100" tucked into the shrubs. Andrew straightened the car and pushed on.

This road was different than any they'd navigated yet. The Honda bumped and bounced and Andrew was forced to reduce speed. Snow covered the uneven ground, which seemed to be dirt and rocks, and probably rarely traveled. The branches overhead made a low canopy, snatching at the car.

"What do I do?" Andrew asked.

"Keep going," Skye said, holding back fear. "It shouldn't be far. Less than a mile."

"What are we looking for?" Ashley asked.

"The directions just read 'END.'"

"Like, end of the world?" Andrew quipped.

Skye tried to think of something funny to say, but her mouth was too dry and her throat too clenched.

The Honda made tentative progress. The tires slipped and grabbed on the uneven surface, pushing persistently along through snow, mud and gravel. Snow fell heavily and Andrew leaned forward in his seat, fighting to see the road through the whiteout.

Skye's mind did flip-flops as she peered into the snow-smeared darkness. Were they in the right place? What if she'd interpreted the numbers wrong? What if there was nothing there? What if there was something there and it was bad?

"How much farther?" Andrew asked.

"I don't know," she managed. "I've lost track. It's hard to tell how far we've gone."

With every push further up the lonely mountain road, Skye grew more uncertain. The woods were dark and impenetrable. How long could a third of a mile be? She was about to tell Andrew to call the whole thing off, turn around, head for Starfish Cove, when a barrier appeared before them.

The board crossed the road, marked with a small sign: "END".

Andrew rolled to a stop and killed the engine. The surroundings fell to an eerie silence. Snowflakes melted softly on warmed glass. The car's headlights shone uselessly into the forest, penetrating only a few feet before being swallowed by darkness.

"Now what?" Andrew asked.

"I have absolutely no idea," said Skye.

In the backseat, Ashley let out a whimper of fear.

FRIDAY, JANUARY 8, 1999
8:22 P.M.

Skye was rigid in her seat, her mind churning with defeat. There was nothing here, nothing but a dark forest and a dead-end road. She must have misinterpreted the map, or made a wrong move.

She'd led two of her favorite people into the middle of nowhere for nothing. Why had she believed this was a good idea? She was such an idiot. She was going to cry, or throw up. They'd have to drive back home, back to the deadly storms and her mother's sadness, having accomplished nothing.

No. There must be an answer here. Skye grabbed her flashlight from her pack and leapt out of the car. She marched around the "END" sign and stomped into the woods. She zipped her coat against the snow and sleet as she moved quickly into the murky forest.

"Skye, wait," her brother called. "Hold on!"

Skye kept going. She found the trail by instinct, barreling through the forest after her bouncing flashlight beam. The forest smelled of pine and something sweeter

173

she didn't recognize, overlaid with the sharp tang of snow. It was much different than the smell of rain. Rain smelled like salt and soil, things of the earth; snow smelled like elements and air, things of the sky. She could smell the mountain itself, the cold scent of stone and ice.

Her Converse were ill-suited for a hike in the snow, but Skye moved so fast her feet hardly touched ground. She flew over downed logs and through muddy patches. Snowflakes collided with her cheeks and caught in her eyelashes.

Ashley and Andrew called for her. Neither had a flashlight, and they would have a hard time following this trail without one. But she didn't feel guilty for leaving them behind. They were safer without her. She didn't know what was ahead, but this was her curse and she would face the consequences alone.

A scent hit and she paused. Wood smoke. Ahead, a glimmer of light. She pushed a branch away and moved on. The glimmer of light became a glowing square—a window. Her flashlight caught the contours of a staircase, a porch, a cabin made of logs. Smoke from a chimney swirled up into the snow and the night sky.

Skye was prepared to walk right up the steps when she paused. Plunks and plops of wet snow fell from the trees to the rooftop and the earth below. Her breath was a whoosh rushing in her ears. Her heart pounded. Skye put her hand on the rail. The wood was wet and cool.

Skye lifted a foot and set it down gently on the first step. She felt like an intruder. But she had been invited here, hadn't she? Summoned, in fact.

Second step, third, one more and she reached the door. From inside, the faint crackle of a fire. From behind, the distant rustle and cry of her brother and best friend working their way through the alpine forest.

Skye's fist raised. Before she could change her mind, she rapped two sharp knocks on the wooden door. Inside, footsteps. A resonant click, an arcing creak, and the door swung open.

A woman stood before Skye. For a disorienting second, Skye looked at her mother. But her mother was 150 miles away. This woman had long blond hair like Skye's own, the opposite of Veronica's dark locks. The woman began to cry, large tears rolling down her pale cheeks. She reached for Skye, pulling her close. She sobbed softly on Skye's shoulder, and Skye hugged her back.

Wood smoke and the scents of the forest were in the woman's hair. Somewhere beneath that were whiffs of the sea and the sand. The woman clung to her and Skye held on too, welling with a deep recognition.

"Penelope," she whispered. "It's you." Skye let the truth of it sink in as she embraced her aunt. "You're not dead."

The woman released from the hug, smoothing Skye's hair and placing her cool palms on Skye's cheeks. Penelope smiled at Skye, her eyes full of tenderness and relief. "Neither are you, my dear."

FRIDAY, JANUARY 8, 1999

8:41 P.M.

Andrew and Ashley dashed up the cabin stairs. Andrew's eyes flitted between Skye and the mysterious woman with the long blond hair.

"Andrew," said Skye. She had one hand on Penelope's arm while the other reached for her brother. "Perhaps you remember your aunt, Penelope."

Andrew's eyes grew wide.

"I'm so glad you made it," Penelope said gently, smiling at Andrew. "Come in from the cold. I'll explain everything. Or at least, everything that I can."

Inside, the room was warm and smelled of something delicious. The three kids hung their wet jackets on hooks by the door and gathered around the small stone fireplace. The hearth was similar to the one in Bertram's cabin, where Skye had spent that long cold night. This hearth, though, was warm and welcoming, the river rock stones heated by a crackling fire.

Penelope ladled hot split pea soup with ham into three bowls and handed them to her guests with hunks of homemade bread. She wore loose pants and a colorful shirt under a long cozy sweater that trailed behind her as she walked. Penelope returned to her chair by the window, and Skye settled into a second overstuffed chair, holding the warm bowl in her lap and spooning the soup into her mouth. Andrew and Ashley sat by the fire on a thick shag rug the color of cranberries. Outside, puffy white flakes fell past the windowpane.

Skye and Penelope shared their starfish stories while Andrew and Ashley listened. Each described the amazing starfish with an eerie blue glowing center. Skye talked of the school field trip and the aquarium, and Penelope of the weeks of storms and the massive tree that fell in her path. Penelope explained how her grandfather, Wolfie, hid her away in this cabin, in fear of what might befall her or their family if she stayed in Starfish Cove.

"Wolfie visited me every couple of months," said Penelope. "But he died only a couple of years after I came here. He made sure I had what I needed before he was gone, and I've been on my own since."

Skye's mind reeled with questions. She barely knew where to begin. "Who painted the starfish in Bertram's cabin?"

"Bertram did."

"And the names on the wall?"

"Bertram wrote the first two—Otto and Alice," said Penelope. "I wrote the second two—Bertram and Heather."

"But your name was up there too," said Skye. "With the numbers that were roads."

"Wolfie did that. Not long before he died, he told me

what he'd added to the wall. He never could bring himself to tell anyone what had happened or where I was. But after I'd been here about a year, he got sick. He knew that he wouldn't be around forever. It made him feel better to know that he'd left behind a clue that I was still alive."

"Why didn't you ever just *leave*?" asked Andrew, who was petting Charlie the cat on the soft rug. "Get the heck out of here and come home?"

"I thought about it," Penelope said. "Hundreds of times. But every time I considered leaving, I imagined the possibility of putting any of you in danger, and I couldn't do it." Penelope rose from her chair. "Let me show you something."

She crossed the room to a tall cabinet. Penelope withdrew a manila envelope from one of the cupboards and returned to her seat. She removed a sheaf of papers and placed it in her lap. "Some of these were gathered by Bertram, some by Wolfie." She selected a paper from the stack and handed it to Skye.

"*Young mother of two vanishes,*" Skye read aloud from what looked to be a Xeroxed copy of a newspaper article. "*February 27, 1962. Heather Beckendorf failed to return from a solo beach walk on Tuesday. Reports of high winds in the area are the only clues left to the grieving family as to what happened to the 30-year-old mother and Starfish Cove resident.*"

Penelope handed Skye another newspaper clipping, this one dated in August of 1945. "*Bertram Beckendorf, age 72, found struck dead by lightning near his home. The old caretaker's cabin for the Hotel Starfish Cove left intact after sudden lightning storm.*"

There were older stories, copied on paper that had yellowed over time. Skye handed each article to Andrew after she'd read it, and he passed it to Ashley. Each revealed few details. Otto was lost at sea; Alice appeared to have frozen to death. The snippets of information were to the point. Life was rugged 100 years ago; accidents happened, people died, no one thought much of it.

A handful of more recent news stories documented the huge storms of 1985, and Penelope's disappearance. Reports traced the search for her after the storm, the authorities' decision to call off the search after a week's time, and the family's sorrow.

Skye held a photo of a young Veronica and David. David's face was grim; Veronica's face was hidden by a curtain of her dark hair. In her arms she clutched a tiny baby. "That's me." Skye traced her finger over the grainy photo that captured the moment in time that had defined her entire life, and Penelope's, too.

Penelope handed over one last clipping. The paper was old and crackly. The small feature appeared to have been torn hastily from its source, with a jagged edge.

The banner was dated October 11, 1915. The heading read *Obituary*.

Skye read aloud. *"Sven Nillson dead at 80. Starfish Cove fisherman Sven Nillson died in his sleep on Tuesday. He was known in his day as a very skillful fisherman, and a competitive one. Nilsson strove to be the most successful fisherman in the region, employing various tactics to drive out would-be rivals. Nillson claimed an ability to use the dark magic of the old country to assist him in his success on the sea. His peers never knew whether to take him seriously, but it was hard to deny that strange occurrences did take place around Old Sven, who frequently boasted that he had the power to charm animals and the force of nature into assisting him eliminate fishing competitors."*

Skye looked at Penelope, startled. "He cursed Otto!" she exclaimed. "All of this is about a fishing rivalry?"

"Fighting over fish and forests are longstanding Oregon traditions," Penelope said wryly. "Throw in one extremely grumpy old wizard, and here we are, 100 years later, carrying around an outdated curse."

"Well, what do we do about it?" Knowing the origin of the curse just made Skye want the starfish out of her life forever.

Penelope looked at the three of them as if this was the question she'd been waiting for. She gazed out the window at the wintry night and the falling snow.

"For a very long time, I believed that doing nothing was the solution." Penelope's face shone beautifully, framed by hair like corn silk. "I believed that hiding on the mountain and guarding all the secrets would keep everyone safe. But things have changed. I reached out to you because you were in danger, and you came here, and I'm grateful.

"But we cannot stay here. We have to go back to Starfish Cove. *I* have to go back to Starfish Cove. We have to face the curse, and we have to do it together. It's probably what should've happened years ago."

Skye believed her aunt's words, even as she was daunted by the idea of facing another unknown challenge. "What will we do when we get there?" she asked.

"I don't know," Penelope admitted, pulling her sweater tight around her shoulders. "Everyone who encountered the starfish before us died, Skye, but you and I have lived. We have to see this as strength, and opportunity. The starfish chose us, perhaps for a reason. If we can find a way to put this curse to rest forever, then that is what we must do. If we think that there is any possibility that we have that power, then we must at least try."

FRIDAY, JANUARY 8, 1999
9:50 P.M.

The hour was late. A bitter wind howled up the mountainside, and through the window, snow blew in a radiant swirl. "Let's get some sleep," said Penelope, rising from her chair. "We'll travel in the morning."

Ashley spoke for the first time in ages. "I need to call my mom." Her voice was small, her face forlorn.

"I don't have a phone, sweetheart," said Penelope.

Ashley's eyes dropped to the floor. Skye said, "Our mom and dad are going to be worried, too."

Penelope nodded in understanding. "We'll leave early in the morning. There's a payphone in Rhododendron." Penelope pulled blankets from a closet, helped her guests settle by the fire, and bid them goodnight.

Despite Skye's qualms about her parents and what was to come, she fell asleep easily. For the first time all week, she didn't dream dark and blustery dreams, full of pulsing blue light and angry winds. Instead, sleeping by the flickering fire in Aunt Penelope's cabin, she dreamt a memory.

The dream was of a day on the beach. The day was one of those summer days on the Oregon Coast that come along so rarely that most people don't believe they exist. But they do, and when they arrive, beach people know you must drop everything and go to the shore. The sky was blue and clear and stretched across the ocean to forever. All day, there wasn't a slice of wind. The air was deliciously warm and smelled of salty sea.

In her dream, Skye was very small. Her pudgy hands swung back and forth as she wobbled down the beach. One hand clutched a small limpet seashell and her toes sank into the sand like gumdrops pushed into cake frosting. Easy waves kissed her feet with gentle splashes. She ran as fast as her small legs could carry her, giggling under a sky that was a million rays of sunshine.

She awoke at dawn to bright light streaming in the window. Skye rose from the nest by the fire and peered outside. The sun reflected between the blue sky and the white landscape, creating an amazing luminescence. The snow looked as if someone had sprinkled it with fistfuls of silver glitter.

Douglas fir trees punctuated the frosty landscape with deep green. At the top of the slope rose the perfect peak of Mt. Hood. Skye was amazed at its beauty.

Penelope came up behind her and placed a hand on Skye's shoulder. "The sun seems like a good omen, doesn't it?"

Skye smiled. "Yes, it does."

Andrew and Ashley had risen and were folding their blankets. Penelope clapped her hands together twice, eagerly. She wore a pair of khaki overalls with her long sweater and a pair of sturdy boots. Her blond curls bounced on her shoulders and she seemed much younger than her years. "Let's get this show on the road! It's been a long time since I had an adventure."

Penelope fed the humans toast with peanut butter and put out two oversized bowls of water and cat food for Charlie, promising him she'd be back soon. She locked up the cabin with an oversized bronze key and gave the front door a little pat. "I'm not saying goodbye," she said to the door. "But you and I have needed a break from each other for quite a while."

Outside, the world looked entirely different than it had the night before. What had been dark and foreboding was now a sunlit postcard-perfect scene. The foursome high-stepped through a few fresh inches of snow, making an easy journey back to the Honda.

"Oh, man." Andrew came to a stop as he regarded the layer of snow covering the small car. The Honda looked pitiful surrounded by the massive winter woods. "That thing barely made it up this mountain. How are we going to get it out of here?"

"We're not," said Penelope. She darted into the woods to a vehicle partially hidden in the trees. It was tall and boxy, painted a deep green. The truck sat high off the ground on sturdy tires, old but solid and meant for snowy mountain roads.

Penelope hopped into the driver's seat and the others followed her, jumping up into the tall vehicle. Penelope said, "I told you Wolfie made sure I had everything I needed before he died. How do you think I got groceries? Or mailed those letters to you, for that matter."

Penelope fired up the engine and masterfully navigated down the snow-packed road. Like the trail through the woods, the road out was a different universe than it had been the night before. The forest was rich and green, and soon they crossed a sparkling river.

They followed the river back to the highway and the National Forest sign that had marked their way in the night. Highway 26 had mostly cleared of snow and Penelope sped up, heading west towards Portland.

"I haven't been past Sandy since 1985," she remarked, grinning like a kid set free from detention.

Rhododendron was the first stop—Penelope pulled into a gas station and handed Ashley a quarter. Ashley galloped across the parking lot and made a call from the payphone. When she returned, she was smiling mischievously.

"What did you tell your mom?" Skye asked.

"I told her I was with you guys, and that we were safe. I told her to call your parents, and to meet us at the aquarium in three hours. Then I hung up on her."

"Why?" asked Penelope, laughing.

"My mom's a journalist. She was going to start asking way too many questions."

Penelope gunned the engine as the truck zoomed west. Skye pulled the map from her backpack, tracing the return route with her finger. They blasted through the mountain town of Sandy, with its ski gear stores, fire station and ice-cream shops. They passed farms and forest as they continued towards the Columbia, which appeared grandly

185

to the right of the highway.

Then it was back through the big city of Portland, the four-lane highways, the traffic, the bridges, the sky-high view of the Willamette and the towering buildings of downtown.

The four of them were quiet, taking in the grandeur and bustle in their own ways, thinking about what was to come. In reverse, and with Penelope at the wheel of her truck, the trip was easy and quick. She may not have been past Sandy in 14 years, but she drove like she had, and soon they were traveling through the farmland and back into the coast range.

The closer they got to Starfish Cove, the quieter everyone became. Penelope's face was the picture of concentration, and Skye wondered what she was thinking. Skye had found more strength within herself in the last few days than she'd ever believed possible, but Penelope's bravery amazed her. Her aunt was returning to a place she hadn't been in well over a decade, a place where everyone believed she was *dead*.

For the last 10 miles of the journey, the ocean was in view to the right. The sun shone here, too, bright and beautiful. Penelope flicked her eyes from the road to the sea. "I missed this place so much." There was sadness in her voice, but peace, too.

Penelope made the right onto Coast without prompting, like a homing pigeon heading to roost. She cruised downhill past the library, past the real estate offices, past the sandwich shop, and took a right turn onto Main Street. She rolled to an easy stop in front of the old blue storefront of the aquarium.

Yellow balloon letters arced over the marquee: "Starfish Cove Aquarium."

"Looks exactly like it did when I was a kid," Penelope said, grabbing her sweater and leaping out of the truck. "Let's go."

SATURDAY, JANUARY 9, 1999

11:04 A.M.

Andrew, Ashley and Skye followed Penelope through the swinging door into the aquarium. A small bell jangled against the glass as they entered. No one was at the front counter.

The foursome strode past a mother with two small children peering at an octopus in a shadowy tank. The next room held tanks of small crabs, anemones and fishes. Through another doorway was the aquarium's back room, home to the touch tank.

"This is where I saw the starfish," Skye said, pointing to a large flat rock in the shallow saltwater. "It's not there," she said in surprise. "It's gone."

"Maybe it's somewhere else in the tank," Ashley offered, poking her fingers under rocks in the tank's corners. Andrew and Penelope looked, too, but the tank was strangely empty—no tiny fish, no scuttling crabs.

A young man appeared through a door. He wore a blue tee shirt adorned with the aquarium logo and carried a walkie-talkie.

"Hey folks," he said. "You have bad timing—the touch tank is temporarily closed."

"What happened?" Penelope asked.

The young man shrugged. "A sick animal. We're not sure what's wrong with it, so we're clearing the tank to make sure none of the other animals are affected. Precautionary measure."

"What kind of animal?" Skye heard her own question as an echo in her head, like someone else had asked it.

"Starfish. It hasn't been with us that long—came in as part of a collection we made last fall. Last night, we noticed it began to appear ill. Now it's lethargic, with off-color flesh. Could be early signs of starfish wasting disease. Are you aware of that condition? The disease has periodically taken out large populations of starfish on the west coast."

Penelope listened politely as the man continued to explain the details of the disease. When he finished, she said, "I don't think this animal has starfish wasting disease. Can I see it, please?"

The man cocked his head. "Are you a veterinarian? Or a wildlife biologist?"

"No. Just a Beckendorf."

Something in Penelope's eyes convinced him. "Wait right here."

He vanished through the door, reappearing a few moments later with a small plastic tub. A bit of water sloshed over the edge as he set it down on a low platform next to the touch table.

"Whoa!" The sight was more astonishing than Skye remembered.

Penelope's eyes were wide-open in awe. "That is simply amazing."

"What?" Andrew was baffled. Ashley's face was knitted in confusion. The young employee looked even more bewildered.

Penelope asked, "Don't you see that?"

"I don't see anything." Ashley shook her head. "Just a starfish."

"You don't see blue?" Penelope spread her fingers in front of her dramatically.

"Blue?" The employee was irritated. He seemed to doubt his decision to show them the starfish. "I suppose this animal is on the grey side of orange, but it is certainly not blue."

"It's so bright," Skye murmured as the starfish emitted a dazzling blue lightshow. The light was more impressive than on Monday. The color pulsed like a hundred lasers from the starfish's center, surrounding the animal with a glowing orb the size of a beach ball. The blue beams danced and swayed, curling towards her like tentacles. "It's beautiful."

"So beautiful," Penelope responded, seeing what Skye did. The three other people in the room wore expressions of confusion and fear.

Captured by the starfish's glow, Skye felt the creature calling for her. But she did not feel afraid.

"May I?" Penelope asked the employee, reaching for the plastic tub and the glowing creature within it.

He shrugged, as if he'd given up trying to figure out what was happening.

Skye was riveted on the starfish as Penelope lifted the animal from the container. The moment her aunt's fingers made contact with the starfish's flesh, the blue light increased in intensity, and the glowing orb grew in size around the animal.

Penelope held the creature in both palms, raising it before her. The iridescent light expanded into an enormous opaque bubble that crept up Penelope's arm and reached her body. Penelope's face was calm and she held the starfish still as the light enveloped her.

Suddenly, Skye knew what to do. She took a deep breath, and stepped into the light.

SATURDAY, JANUARY 9, 1999

11:28 A.M.

Skye moved towards Penelope and placed her hands over the starfish, tucking her fingers around the animal in Penelope's hands. Together, they embraced the starfish.

The starfish's flesh was rough and cool, firm but pliable, and a pulsing energy traveled from the animal into her body. The iridescent blue orb grew even larger in response to their combined touch, encircling Skye and Penelope entirely, surrounding them with a fabulous sparkling light. Penelope's eyes shone bright blue, as Skye imagined did her own.

Skye and Penelope lifted the starfish towards the sky. The animal remained still, but energy coursed from it beyond, filling Skye with warmth and a curious feeling of strength.

Penelope smiled at Skye and took in a deep breath, basking in the light around them. Blue beams of light bounced off of Penelope's blond curls as the circle grew larger still. She gazed up to the starfish for a long moment, and finally, she spoke.

"Starfish. It is time for you to be free." Her voice was peaceful and kind. "You have spent over 100 years entrapped in service to a dark spell that was never your own. We release you, and we release our family, from this curse."

The blue light sparked and jumped from the starfish's center. The animal's flesh contracted and its legs tensed. Skye repeated Penelope's words, "Starfish. It is time for you to be free. We release you, and we release our family, from this curse."

Light popped off of the starfish, flying about them in whirling molten flashes as the starfish contracted further and the orb's surface buckled and swayed.

Penelope and Skye held fast, repeating together this time, "Starfish. We release you, and we release our family, from this curse."

Blue light exploded around Penelope and Skye, zapping and pulsing. The starfish became very heavy in their hands. The iridescent bubble expanded further, filling the room, everything glowing blue and crackling with white fire.

The starfish became leaden and hot, and Penelope and Skye bent under the pressure, struggling to keep the animal aloft. Just when it seemed that they would collapse, that the expanding blue orb would overtake everything, the circle of light contracted with a quick snap. The iridescence compressed into the starfish, shimmering in an intense blue spot before disappearing altogether with a white-hot pop.

Penelope and Skye unlaced their hands and showed

their palms to each other. They held nothing. The light was gone. The starfish was gone.

Penelope drew Skye in and wrapped her arms around her. Skye hugged her aunt for a long moment before turning towards the other people in the room. She threw her arms around Andrew, and then Ashley, and then even the aquarium employee. All three of them hugged her back, their faces still cloaked in confusion.

"What just happened?" Andrew finally asked timidly.

"Didn't you see it?" Skye felt all of the energy of the last few minutes coursing through her body. "The explosion of light, the glowing starfish, all of that *blue*?"

Andrew shook his head. "Nope." Ashley nodded her head in agreement with him.

"All I saw—I think," said Andrew, "—was your starfish friend vanish into thin air." Ashley looked entirely overwhelmed. The aquarium employee blinked and took a few steps backwards.

Skye was undaunted. She bounced up and down on her toes. "That was awesome!" She danced over to Penelope, whose face was a vision of happiness, and threw her arms around her again.

The bells on the aquarium's exterior door jangled. A beat later, into the room walked Jerry, Linda, Veronica and David.

The parents acted first. Veronica leapt across the room and grabbed Skye and Andrew. Tears coursed down her face as she clung to them both. David joined her, embracing his family with a big bear hug. Linda wrapped her arms around Ashley, growling in her ear, "I never thought you'd

194

be a runaway. Don't do it again."

Jerry watched the scene with a tinge of a smile. He sidled over to the aquarium employee and said, "How's your day going?"

"It's been a little weird," the employee replied.

Next to the employee stood a woman in overalls and a colorful knit sweater. Jerry stuck out his hand and she took it. "I'm Jerry Petrichor, KTSC. Do you work here?"

"No," she replied, smiling. "Nice to meet you. My name is Penelope Beckendorf."

Jerry's eyes grew wide as he clamped down on Penelope's hand, pumping it up and down and unable to speak a word.

At the sound of Penelope's voice, Veronica unraveled herself from her family and turned to face her sister. For a suspended moment, she stood in shock, deciding whether to trust her own eyes.

Penelope met Veronica's gaze. Heavy tears spilled down her cheeks, the mirror of those sliding down Veronica's face and into her dark curly hair.

The sisters stepped towards each other, colliding into a hug that lasted for a very long time. Their hair swirled around their shoulders, mixing together, dark meeting light, until the two entangled into one.

WEDNESDAY, JULY 7, 1999
1:31 P.M.

Through the KTSC window, the sky was blue and clear and stretched across the ocean to forever. It was one of those summer days that come along so rarely on the Oregon Coast that most people don't believe they exist. But they do, and when they arrive, beach people know you must drop everything and go to the shore.

But first, Skye and Jerry had work to finish up.

"Stormy," Jerry called. In the six months that Skye had been an intern at the station, Jerry had adopted her family's nickname for her. "How's tonight's segment coming along?"

"Good," Skye replied. "Almost finished."

After that amazing moment in the aquarium back in January, a lot had changed. A few days after the starfish disappeared, the whole group had gathered at the Happy Oyster to celebrate Skye's 14th birthday. Sitting across from Jerry, Skye had finally worked up the nerve to not only talk to him, but to tell him about her interest in meteorology. He suggested she come and work with him at the station a few afternoons a week.

Now that it was summer, she spent time at KTSC nearly every day. At first, she'd done basic research, tracking weather patterns, understanding atmospheric systems, guessing at forecasts, learning as she went. But as she progressed, Skye began researching historical weather events — very specific events, in fact. At Jerry and Linda's urging, Skye dove into her family's unique history with weather in Starfish Cove. The three of them put together a special series about the strange story of the starfish and the death and destruction it left in its wake. The series aired in segments. Tonight was part 8, "The Day the Creek Flooded."

Skye made a few small edits to the video file and hit "save." She walked to Jerry's desk, where he jotted notes about tomorrow's weather forecast for the evening broadcast. "How about you?" she asked him.

"It's a wrap," he said. "Let's get out of here."

Skye glanced at the clock — only 2, which meant a few hours before they had to be back here for the 5 o'clock news. Leaving their jackets behind, the two exited through the metal door of the old cinder block station and walked west across the parking lot. As they climbed the loose sand of the dune, the beach grass swayed gently in the cool breeze and the sun was warm on their skin. They crested the top of the dune and there it was — the glorious Pacific Ocean. White-tipped waves rolled easily onto the beach, leaving behind a brushstroke of water-darkened sand with every fluid swipe. In the air were the scents of salt, seaweed and the burnt wood of last night's beach fire.

Skye knelt and untied her Converse, slipping them off, and her socks too. She gave her jeans a couple of folds at the ankle and dug her toes into the smooth sand. When she stood again, she caught sight of Ashley, who leapt and waved from down the beach, at a wide spot before the Old Docks. They jogged towards the group of coolers, beach chairs, and people.

Veronica and Penelope sat side by side, their hair tossing about in the breeze like black and white kites flown side by side. David and Andrew stood barefoot, throwing a blue Frisbee, laughing as it caught on a gust and dove into the surf as often as it landed in hand. Ashley ran between them, trying to intercept the Frisbee from the guys but mostly splashing into the surf to retrieve it for them. Linda sat near Veronica and Penelope, holding a book in her lap.

Skye plopped onto the sand at her mother and aunt's feet and lay on her back, closing her eyes against the bright summer sun. After the events of January, Penelope had remained in Starfish Cove. She stayed with the Clancys for a while, but only until she finished the renovations to Bertram's cabin. Penelope had taken on the project with enthusiasm, and the whole family had chipped in to help her fix up the small home. They had worked to clear the old Starfish Cove Resort road, which led to the cliff-top, so that she could drive her truck to the cabin. They'd nailed up fallen boards, cleaned dusty corners and brought in cheery furnishings, which transformed the place into a great little house, perfect for one.

Penelope had painted the cabin inside and out, but she left Bertram's starfish on the bedroom wall, along with the names, dates and road numbers that had led Skye to her. Penelope said she would never dream of painting over the art. That was her story.

Outside, they planted a memorial garden of rhododendrons and hyacinths. Andrew made a wooden sign to nail to the garden fence—it read: "In Memoriam of The Dead Beckendorfs."

Penelope waited tables at the Happy Oyster, where David had become a full time chef. He flourished in his new job, loving every minute of creating delicious meals for the Oyster's guests.

Veronica poked Skye in the side with her toe, and Skye squinted up at her mother, smiling and giving her a little wave. Since Penelope's return, the sisters had spent tons of time together, and Veronica's moods had become much lighter. Skye had come to accept that her mother would always have dark moments, times when she slipped into blackness and became quiet and withdrawn. But putting to rest the mysteries of her mother and sister had brought her peace.

Both sisters wished sometimes that Wolfie had made different choices with the secrets he'd carried and the actions he took. How might things have been different if he'd been able to trust the family with the truth, to have faith that together, they could figure out what to do? But the past was the past, and Veronica and Penelope took heart in the fact that the mysteries had been brought to light eventually. Not knowing anything was always the hardest state to bear.

The family had plans to return to the Mt. Hood cabin

later in the summer, to see where Penelope had been all of those years. Back in January, David and Andrew had returned to retrieve the Honda, Charlie the cat, and a few of Penelope's things, but this time, the whole family would go. Linda, Jerry and Ashley would join them. The trip was Veronica's idea. She wanted to reclaim that place, for Penelope and for the family, as one of unity and celebration instead of isolation and fear.

Skye lay on her back in the sunshine. Her family and friends laughed and played over the crash of the ocean. The warmth of the sand on her back and the cyclic sound of the waves rolling onto the beach soothed her, and she was warm and relaxed.

A lot had happened in Starfish Cove this year, some of which made her wish to be somewhere else. But Skye couldn't imagine living in any other place. She would leave for college one day, but she would return to forecast the weather right here in her hometown. From the storm that had marked her birth, to the events of last January, to whatever may come in the future, this was her story, and this was where she was supposed to be. Like all of the Beckendorfs before her, Skye was born to stand on the shores of the Oregon Coast, with her toes rooted in the sand and her arms reaching for the sky.

The End

Kim Cooper Findling is a fifth-generation Oregonian and award-winning writer and editor of stories about her beloved home state. She is the author of *Bend, Oregon Daycations: Day Trips for Curious Families, Day Trips From Portland: Getaway Ideas for the Local Traveler* and *Chance of Sun: An Oregon Memoir.* For the last two decades, she has worked as a magazine editor, travel writer, memoirist, journalist, teacher and author from Bend, Oregon. See kimcooperfindling.com.

Libby Findling is a sixth-generation Oregonian and a student in Bend, Oregon. She is an accomplished actor, musician, comedienne, writer and storyteller. She loves rivers, rain, wandering the forests of Oregon and jamming out to some funky bops. In the future, she hopes to create songs, films, and more books.